# Light is Parasite

**Cover art by Michael Hall**

First Edition
© Copyright 2024 Peter Turner Farrar All rights reserved

# Chapter 1 – Grief is Prose, not Poetry.

Darkness crept around the room, there was not the slightest glint or spark, all light banished.

Rolling over in bed, Tij stretched out tentatively through the cold empty side. She reached across the crumpled sheets, her open hand paused, and slowly clenched.

The room did not buzz, hiss, creak, or bang, Tij saw to that, it was hermetically silent. Tij sighed as she struck her head back deep into the pillows, sinking slightly into the soft bed as she reached over to the empty side one last time as a scream echoed through the house.

Tij clapped her hands once, a sharp pain coursed from her right hand. She clenched it into a fist, the agony caused her to shudder, but she bit her lip to keep from crying out. The index finger had a deep cut all the way down to the thumb, blood had congealed in places but the wound bled freely around it.

The sound of the hands coming together, one severed one intact, triggered a response in the walls and ceiling around her, changing from opaque to clear. Tij squeezed her eyes closed and stretched out her arms. She felt the light growing in intensity through closed eyelids, its searing white brilliance all in shades of flesh and blood.

The light continued to increase, white light woven from every colour, a flood that surrounded her, and then at a rate that never failed to take her breath away, she felt the slender border between her and the light dissolve.

Twisting from the comfort of her bed away from the blood-soaked empty side of the sheet, Tij swung her legs over and reached for the floor with her toes. The world can remain unseen in absolute light as well as total darkness and the necessary rituals in searching for any solid thing within either place was disappointingly the same.

When fully lit, the bedroom was no longer a solace, it was just a room. Tij looked around at the sparse furniture; there was the bed itself, the bedside table, a tall wooden wardrobe, and a single chair in the corner. Standing in the light, Tij moved toward the glass wall closest to her, perfectly clear it magnified the light from outside, and held up her ruined hand to shield her eyes.

Blood dripped onto the floor as sharp pain set fire to the nerves along her arm. Tij clenched and opened her hand in rapid succession, wincing as the deep wound opened and closed, external pain was somehow much easier to cope with and left a scar all could see and empathise with. She watched as her wound fizzed where it touched the light.

The flesh grew around the nerves filling in the gaps at first with blood, muscle, and tendon, finally the skin was replaced. If only all pain and loss could be cured so easily.

She took a quick, cold shower, washing the blood away, there was no scar on her hand or anywhere else on her body, her flesh was a lie; turning away from her own reflection, Tij dried herself vigorously with the rough towel then folded it carefully away before moving to the wardrobe, flicking through her sparse, colourful belongings until settling on a red woollen knee-length dress with long sleeves. Tij pulled on the formal attire that identified her as redemption.

Tij left the bedroom turning toward the sitting room at the centre of the house. This room was warm and dishevelled, a testament to a long life. Tij ran her hand on the tattered armchair placed between two large bookcases full of dog-eared books, magazines and scraps of paper held together by whatever served that purpose: elastic bands, string, or ribbon. Two sofas, worn to threads, sat upon a carpet that had lost all its colour. There was still blood here; Tij did not want the drones cleaning anything in this room, this was a solace, it was not to be interfered with.

Everything was covered in a light layer of dust and sat in its proper place, everything here belonged, all these precious relics came from a single life, a life that did not end, this room was a reliquary of all the bright, potent moments she had shared with so many, a sacred place dedicated to all those she had lost. Here were the big moments, the times that held the greatest emotion, the times that stood out in her immortal life, all testaments to her existence, and these meticulously curated tokens were individual evidence of a love and a life once shared. The room was full to bursting, every corner was piled high with paper boxes and folders, every bookcase and shelf covered with bundles of letters of all sizes, keepsakes and mementos eclectically grouped together, all worn and cared for.

The world was on a constant journey toward reset, but Tij yearned for it to stay the same. She walked along the short corridor that led deeper into the house; there were three doors on either side, only one was closed.

Tij walked to the closed door. The corridor had no natural light and the bulbs flickered slightly as she placed her hand on the wooden frame, sliding down to the cool handle, sticky with blood, which she turned and then entered.

The room had no windows but was brilliantly lit. It was set into the structure at the centre of the house and was the first of countless rooms that delved into the foundations below. In this room, Tij kept the last person who loved her.

Tij was struck by a searing blow to the head. She reeled away as she shielded her eyes from the burning heat. Her eyes were still adjusting to the bright, burning form of her lover, who was ablaze in orange light and muttering to herself as she prowled around the wreckage of the room, still holding the shard of broken mirror she had used to attack Tij the last time she had entered.

Holding out her new hand in entreaty seemed only to anger the bright form that sprung like a feral cat toward her, slashing the air wildly with the shard as she screamed all her pain, desperation and hate toward Tij.

Tij skilfully avoided the attack, her lover was in a weakened state caused by the memories she fought to hold onto, memories that caused her body to burn until they were given release by redemption.

'Please stop, Enid, it's me, please.' The last word was lost in a deep sob.

The heat in the room was unbearable. Tij circled her burning lover carefully, avoiding the wreckage of their life together. The room was heavy with the scent of scorched sweat as Tij's eyes adjusted to the brightness emanating from Enid who now stood motionless, clutching the glass shard in one hand. It was then Tij heard the blood drip onto the floor from a wound that could not be seen in the burning flesh.

'I know you,' Enid hissed, the features of her face lost in light. 'You are the one who says she loves me, the one who won't let me go.'

Tij moved a single step closer to Enid.

'You wanted to stay; do you remember?'

'Of course I remember,' snarled Enid. 'That's why I burn.' In a flurry of movement, she cut across her chest and face, across her arms, and then threw the glass against the wall behind Tij. Enid then opened her arms wide as sizzling blood fell from her onto the floor in thick heavy drops.

'Haven't I suffered enough for you? All I have is pain; memory is pain. Why do you let me burn, please ... please.' She dropped to her knees and began to cry. Tij thought she could hear the tears hiss on her scorched flesh.

Standing, Tij moved tentatively toward Enid, carefully treading through the broken items, curated from their life together and now strewn around the room; each one mattered, each one represented precious reminders of their life together.

In the beginning, Enid desperately wanted to hold onto her agonised life, and Tij loved her for that. Enid wanted to hold onto the memories of their life together so badly that she was willing to go through torture to keep them.

Even now, Enid knelt in the part of the room where there was the highest concentration of intact memorabilia: photographs, books, the minutiae of life down to the cutlery they had used the first time they met. Memory was pain but still Enid cherished them.

Tij fell to her knees next to Enid. Despite her closeness, all she could see was a human form glowing brightly, no features could be discerned, it had been so long since she had seen Enid smile, her deep blue eyes, full lips, and short red hair that felt like velvet.

Enid was already in agony when she had first asked Tij for redemption, so long ago.

This was like a physical blow to Tij, her lover was asking to leave her, and the method of her escape would be Tij herself, Tij would give her redemption, as she did to everyone in the world. She would have to take the very essence of the person she loved within her, feel what she felt, then Enid would be gone, her like never seen again. The exact configuration of experience and personality that was Enid would never be seen again.

Enid was in this room in part to keep her out of sight of the star. When Enid, or anyone burning from memory, caught sight of the star it would magnify any pain they felt; it was a punishment for holding onto a life the star needed to consume. Tij had moved her to the only place in their home that had no windows or external walls and she had filled the room with everything they had gathered in a life all too brief. Here, Tij was applying the lessons she had learnt from those who had tried to hold onto their memories. They had all failed, but hope is a venal thing. This room was full of evidence of their life together, moments shared and enjoyed, the bright relics of a life lived both separately and entwined. It had worked at first, this cocoon offered Enid a distraction from her pain, letting her shift focus from the unrelenting agony as she drifted around the memories and objects of her and Tij's life together.

Enid had fought like no other that Tij had ever loved before, and each day won from oblivion was a blessing until the pain became too much, and then it slowly became a curse. That was a long time ago.

Tij put her arms around Enid, her skin burnt and was wet with blood. She winced but kept hold.

Enid tensed and rocked from side to side in Tij's embrace, whispering into her ear repeatedly, 'Please, please, there is nothing but pain, please, Tij, if you love me, please take the pain away.' Enid was lost in agony, soaked in sweat, blood and tears.

These fragments of a shattered life that she had placed around Enid did not comfort her lover as Tij intended, these consolations from a life well-lived, the memories they held offered no respite, instead they magnified her pain and misery.

Enid wanted to stay, Tij knew this, she had promised she would endure, suffer to any extent to stay with her. This proved to Tij beyond doubt that she loved her, but what she was certain of would soon be tested beyond doubt, because soon all that was Enid would be swept up to be held within Tij, it would be their final moment of intimacy. This was what Tij was, she was redemption, she brought the end so the world could begin again.

Tij held Enid tightly, feeling her breath on her neck and her skin scorch as she squeezed her lover close. All she needed to do to redeem someone was simply to take their hand, but she loved Enid, and such a gesture would not be enough. Before letting her go forever she would hold her close. Goodbyes are unavoidable, recognising when it is the right time does not make it easier. Tij's choice was to release Enid, who had fought so hard to stay with her. Tij would take her pain, she would take all that she was, all they were together.

Pulling Enid closer, Tij reached for the essence of her lover with her own, passing through their scorched connected flesh that prickled and coursed with fire and razor-edged light. Both were shivering uncontrollably; Enid from relief, a sudden draining of an infected wound that her memories had become, Tij from shock, she was struggling to breathe, lost in the constellation that was Enid. The gravity of redemption drew each spark toward her, to the core of her being set aside for this purpose. The constellation was all the colours of Enid, all her fear and sadness, defiant flecks of joy sparkling in between panic and pain, and in that instant, Tij knew everything about the woman she loved every part of her being was laid bare. Fierce were motes thrown into the void inside Tij, and for an instant it was the shape of Enid, every thread a moment lived and remembered, cooling, glowing gently, finally pulsing like a heartbeat, it was a perfect truth.

Tij's core began to pull on the constellation, warping the form of Enid a mote at a time, the gravity of her own grief forcing the constellation into an accretion disk, one mote at a time. Time here passed slowly though not even a second had passed as Enid's form was lost. Tij screamed, her desperation given force, but there was no sound, no one to hear, the only effect was the impact to the constellation, the ripple of the screams serving only to quicken the disruption to the constellation. Enid's bright form was lost completely, all that she was now – an accretion disk of disembodied memories, nothing cohesive, a life shattered through the prism of redemption into dust and sparks.

Tij drew each memory toward her, moments of sadness and pain fell first, heavier elements so easily drawn to oblivion, joy was gossamer thin, slowly drawn to redemption, but as it hit Tij's core it was joy that left the deepest scars.

All that was Enid had now been taken, her light now resting in the place Tij kept at her centre, the place where everyone on the sphere had taken redemption before. The end is never special, it is not unique, even if the person truly is.

Tij shivered uncontrollably, as the echoes of her misery ran along ancient, tarnished nerves, amplified by the heavy presence of Enid that now sat in the heart of her.

With practised despair, she steered her misery away from the beloved essence resting within her. This grief was for her, she did not want Enid to feel it, to react.

Tij would remember, and not forget, she would never forget Enid, she never forgot anyone. Holding the one she loved in a full embrace, Tij whispered over and over that she loved her, but she knew Enid was gone, it was a life she had ended, it was a mercy, but it felt like betrayal.

Who Tij still held was no longer glowing, but she still bled from wounds that could now be seen now the light had died. What remained looked like Enid, but all she was, all she had been, was now taken from her and rested inside Tij. What was left was ruined, malleable flesh, an empty vessel, she was now grinning in her absence of memory, devoid of soul.

Tij released her embrace. Grief and anger, mixed with a flash of revulsion, was forged into the heavy, sharp weight that settled itself at the core of her. This was Enid now, this was where she really was, an essence taken deep inside of Tij, for her to transport like cargo to be offered as fuel to the star.

Getting to her feet, Tij steadied herself on the wall of the room as she slipped in the wreckage of the memories of their lives. She looked at Enid, who was grinning at her from a vacant, severed face.

Enid's hands fell to her side and Tij could see the scars, some old, others deep and new, still bleeding. Looking closer, Tij could see the wounds were all over Enid's body.

'When did you do this, why didn't you tell me?' Tij asked Enid, her voice strained.

Enid looked at her and continued to grin inanely.

Tij took her hand and felt along her scars with her fingers, smearing blood across Enid's pale, bruised flesh.

Fury filled Tij as she kicked out at the relics of their life in the room, the photographs, souvenirs, and trinkets. She leant down, picking fistfuls of broken material and throwing them against the walls that enclosed them, and then a nullifying stillness fell upon her, and she wiped away tears with the back of her hand.

Breathing deeply, Tij searched the debris for anything that could be salvaged. She chose a photograph of them both taken during one of the many festivals, and a small journal filled with watercolours and sketches that Enid treasured. Lastly, Tij found a bracelet, woven from willow and red ribbon. She collected these precious objects and placing them in a box on the table with the few items already there, she closed the lid and placed the box, bearing Enid's name, onto one of the shelves with all the others bearing the names of those she had loved.

Standing behind her was what remained of Enid, who looked at her but seemingly did not recognise her. She was beautiful, even covered in blood, sodden red hair and vacant dark blue eyes, and she was grinning, but there was no personality behind it, it was an empty grin and Tij felt both grief and revulsion in equal measure.

Tij grabbed the husk that was her lover by the hand, her scorched hand holding Enid's scarred one, and led her from the room. Enid followed with no resistance as she was led through the house. Tij paused in the corridor as she took in the careful curation of their life together that was the living room, a tattered eulogy of their love. She winced as she looked back into the room they had just left, here was how they ended, scorched wreckage and hidden scars.

Tij would lead her like she had led everyone else she had ever given redemption to, where they would all stand grinning, all adrift in the absence of memory.

As she opened the door to their home and out into the sphere, Tij gently led Enid through into the blinding light.

As her eyes adjusted, Tij looked out at the world wrapped around the burning star at its centre. As soon as her flesh touched the light, Enid's scars began to heal, scabs of fizzing diamonds covered the wounds then fell away, leaving her pale skin unblemished, renewed.

Tij did not see Meco approach. He creased his scarred face into a scowl before he opened his mouth to speak.

'We all have to make sacrifices.' Meco's voice was dry and stern as he looked at Enid.

'It's not a sacrifice if you have no choice,' Tij replied through clenched teeth, her grief almost nullifying her anger.

Meco was looking down at his ruined hands, running one across the deep scars that made up his face. This deliberate act angered Tij.

'See what I have given, see what I always give?' She pulled the grinning Enid around to face him.

Meco looked at Enid, his eyes were rheumy.

'She is joy-struck, free from memory and the pain it causes; she is one of the Blissed,' Meco said coolly, and stared at Tij, waiting.

Tij stared back at Meco for long moments. He was without feeling, merciless, a tool that served the star, they both did. There was nothing to say, this conversation had happened so many times before, and Meco did not care,

Throughout their conversation Tij never released Enid's hand. Meco was watching as she turned toward the path that led away from her house. She took just four steps then stopped.

'We need one more to complete the harvest.'

# Chapter 2 – The Road as Prey.

Watching Tij walk away, hand in hand with Enid, her shoulders shaking from sobbing, Meco ground his teeth as he caught a fly mid-air without taking his eyes from Tij. Feeling it struggle between his index finger and thumb, feeling the insect squirm helplessly, he carefully placed the fly in one of the many webs on the low wall surrounding Tij's home.

'Sacrifice,' Meco sneered as he shook his head in irritation. 'Succumbing to the inevitable is not sacrifice.'

He looked at Tij as she led the shell that was Enid by the hand and mused. You are consistently cruel, and you are loved – I am occasionally brutal, and I am feared.

Neither he nor Tij were machines, not in the true sense of the word, but their purpose was as inescapable as any programming. The only difference between them and the other mechanisms that served the sphere was that they felt the passage of time, and the wounds it inflicts.

Meco stared at the star at the centre of the world that was wrapped around its constant yellow glare in an enclosed sphere. He felt the heat and light warm his ruined flesh. The star was fuelled by memories sacrificed to it, some willingly so, some not, it was those that did not that concerned Meco.

'It isn't a sacrifice if you have no choice.' He repeated Tij's words to himself and clenched his fists in anger as he screamed after Tij: 'My life is my sacrifice, and I have no choice.' He watched for any reaction, she neither slowed down or turned to face him.

He kicked the bag that lay open between his black-booted feet. Looking down, Meco followed the road beneath him, up toward the concave horizon. Squinting in the harsh, constant light, he stepped once to the right so that it led up perfectly behind the star. The road looped away from him in a perfect circle, up behind the star, above them both, behind him and inevitably back beneath his feet.

Meco crouched down and searched the bag, grabbing a pair of thick, worn work gloves and a roll of tape. His mind did not retain anything that did not serve his purpose; he did not remember so he dreamt, and he could only sleep when the harvest was complete. Meco needed a world empty of people, truly silent before he could rest.

He carried the aches and pains of an impossibly long and hard life. Once the harvest was complete, he would return home, and dreams and isolation would be his reward.

Pulling on the gloves, Meco clapped his hands together, stepping back as most of the dust slowly fell to the floor. He quickly rubbed away any of the dust that settled on his black boilersuit.

First the harvest needed to be completed, the star's appetite was endless, everyone but Tij and himself lost themselves to it eventually. There were the Blissed, who were keen to shed a bright, short life relishing the opportunity of becoming something new, eager to slip into a new form and existence, which they wore like clothing and then cast aside the moment it began to hurt. Some ran and concealed themselves away in the hidden places of the world; it was his purpose to hunt them and bring them to redemption.

He named his prey Seeds. Whereas he considered the Blissed willing cattle, the Seeds were grain, propagated by desperation and nourished by the memories they suffered to keep.

Desperation is an odd thing; it felt intensely personal, but like everything else it is just a habit. Meco understood this because he needed to. Awareness of their suffering was simply knowledge that helped him find the ones he hunted. It was not empathy, such a thing would require a similar experience to compare, all Meco had was his purpose, his role.

Meco wrapped the base of his gloves in tape, biting of the excess and smoothing it carefully down, then did the same at the base of his boilersuit, sealing any gap between. One more Seed was all that was needed to complete the harvest.

His prey was easy to track, pain made them reckless, a pain caused by memories they refused to sacrifice to the star to be burnt away and their forms reforged. The paths the Seeds fled along were clumsy and well-trodden, entirely predictable, an eternal recurrence.

Zipping up the bag, Meco thrust an arm through each handle and jumped slightly to settle the weight on his back.

The entire surface of the sphere sat upon an endless matrix of rooms long buried by a living world, soil and stone was often surmounted by a building, a pinnacle that broke the surface. The streets were a line of these escarpments, jutting up, and these formed the towns of the world, only one of which remained fully intact, the other was in ruins and long abandoned.

Where his prey chose to hide told Meco a great deal about the Seed he was hunting. It indicated the level of resistance he could expect, and he would prepare, failure hurt like memory.

Meco turned from the path that circumvented the sphere and followed a well-worn trail through long grass until he approached the edge of a copse. He paused and stood still beneath the first tree staring at the shadows at his feet, he rarely allowed his mind to wander but here he became struck by an unbidden epiphany; light is parasite, and we are its shadow.

The tree he stood beneath, half scorched from an unremembered storm, its leaved branches providing the better shade, was where he sheltered from the constant light.

He compared his own small shadow to that of the tree. Looking up, he saw the star burning at the centre of the world immediately overhead, irrevocably present.

Meco knew he would never cast a larger shadow, his would always be underfoot and small, not a thing in of itself, but held within greater things. He had never been loved, even the word itself was alien, but it was something he had learnt from one of the objects cast from the engine to the surface, objects avidly sought out by the Seeds.

He put his hand in his pocket and pulled out a pen, unremarkable but well-used. He pressed it against his bare scarred cheek. The contact with his skin flashed an image in his mind, it was a memory, but it did not belong to him, so it had no weight, no substance, but it was something at least, a distraction, a soft moment in a hard life.

His mind spun as his senses switched to align with the memories imbued in the pen, and then he was somewhere else.

'Wake up,' a gentle low voice said, and he felt warm lips brush his.

He opened his eyes and smiled, a smile a dark-haired woman returned as she grabbed his hands and climbed on top of him, leaning forward, pushing his hands down on either side, causing her to lean forward when she kissed him again. Her long dark hair fell around his face, shadowing him from the light that encircled them.

'In a world of light, this is the only shadow I seek,' he said, but it wasn't his voice.

He could see the mischief in her eyes as she moved her face toward him, then she stopped, it was not just movement, but the feel of her body on top of his, the sound of the sheets as they moved, everything stopped, the memory had ended.

Meco did not understand the feelings this image evoked, he had no memory of his own, but he knew, even if what he felt was borrowed, it was all he had.

Shaking his head, Meco felt himself return from the distraction of the memory the pen contained. He looked to the sphere above and around him, looking for what he knew, the familiar paths, and his senses began to attune back to stark reality.

'The world encloses the star, one inside the other, and the harvest feeds its bright heart. In orbit around the star the engine ranged in between star and sphere, providing the link between the two, its purpose to provide the harvest, the fuel for the star to ensure continuance.' Meco repeated this over and over until he felt himself fully returned.

Not all objects held memories, those that did were always found in the same places, sown to the world by a robot that inhabited the engine, which orbited the star. They were cast onto the same parts of the sphere, fields full of everyday objects dripping with memory.

This was where the Seeds found themselves irresistibly drawn. It was in such places that Meco would lie in wait for them. Every predator had hunting grounds.

A time-worn trail seldom lies, and it had brought Meco through the copse to the outskirts of one of the abandoned towns. Hearing a loud shout that was unintelligible, he slipped behind a tree. Kneeling down he closed his eyes, locating the general direction of the sound. He then peered cautiously around the trunk to identify its source. In the street opposite, two doors down to his left, stood a man in the doorway who was singing at the top of his voice in a rough timbre, stopping only to sob, or occasionally mutter, to himself.

The thin man, dressed in the remnants of the provided attire – dark trousers, t-shirt, but shoeless, he was glowing. Burning things cast no shadow, they create them.

This Seed was collecting items from the ground that had been strewn from the engine. Meco understood why, each item was drenched with pollution not needed by the star: a thought, sometimes a daydream or feeling, occasionally a work of some kind, a song, a story, or an image of strange places. All components of lives lived, all filled with heavy emotions like grief, sadness, or anger, like the pen he had in his pocket, which as beautiful as it was, ached with a deep sadness, it was an emotion Meco felt but did not understand.

The potent feelings each object contained were distractions, gathered by the Seeds to shift the focus away from their own pain even for just a moment, or rarely it would help them to understand it.

The gathered objects would be taken by the Seeds to a hidden place where it would be used to build a cocoon, a shell of random, discarded things that together blended into stories, thoughts, images, or music, which worked as a salve against the unrelenting pain and the pull of redemption.

Meco watched as the Seed picked up object after object, pausing over each, lost in whatever the object held, sometimes for seconds, sometimes minutes at a time. The Seed proceeded to discard some objects while keeping others.

Once he was satisfied with the selection he had gathered, either stuffed into pockets or held in clumsy arms, he resumed singing, which dropped occasionally into a nervous hum to fill the gaps of a near forgotten or misremembered tune.

He never finished a song, the Seed was lost in his own pain, he could not focus, he sung or uttered whatever popped into his head, regardless of context. The Seed then stooped to pick up one more object, Meco could not see what it was, adding it to the carefully curated pile held in his arms. He then walked toward a doorway and went inside.

Meco crept cautiously from the shadows of the trees, dropping the bag onto the floor, then checking the tape and his uniform one last time for any gaps. Satisfied, he sighed and followed the Seed to what was a rusted metal house leaning heavily into a pointed rock cave.

Ruined things rarely seemed to shine, Meco thought briefly. The metal house had long since collapsed in on itself, the roof now lying upon the second floor, which was split in two revealing the cellar below. Meco stood at the entrance and listened.

He could hear the tuneless hum of the Seed, it was fleeting, but it was there. It was a song, half-known but well-loved. Meco looked more closely at the debris around him. He could see planks and wrecked furniture that had been moved aside to reveal a gap in the wall just large enough for someone to pass through.

Easing his way in, he wore silence like clothing. Meco stood in a cellar where he could see, in the walls around him, three tunnels dug through the brick into the darkness beyond. He closed his eyes and listened at each tunnel in turn.

None were silent; the tunnel in front of him echoed with laughter, the one to his left reverberated with screams and the one to his right carried the shapeless hum uttered by the Seed.

The tunnels themselves were new, dug through old walls, a change to the very fabric of the world brought about by the need to escape it.

Meco did not know where the rooms below the sphere came from, and he had explored many, but he knew what soil was, it was layer upon layer of decaying living matter. The grass, the trees, were all dependent on what went before. All roots were dug into the past from which they gained nourishment and strength, all necessary to live in an unyieldingly bright world. Life sprung from the soil, but it always sought the light. The Seeds were an exception, emerging from their solace only to collect objects, or to surrender to the star's will, but they shunned the light wherever possible.

He did not know the number of Seeds on the sphere, as each harvest completed, the paucity of willing Blissed meant he would need to hunt more of them than before, he would drag them kicking and screaming toward redemption. Some fought with vicious and manic desperation, others folded and complied. He could never tell which, not with certainty. Where they hid told him much, but it was often still unpredictable, all Meco knew was that there was a minimum number of Blissed that needed taking to redemption, or the harvest would not meet the necessary amount, and the world would not renew, and he could not have that. It was an obsession; he needed his rest. He faced the uncertain darkness in front of him so that he could dream later, and so he followed the sound of the broken tune of his prey down the tunnel.

The rooms below the surface varied a great deal, from little more than holes in the ground to others that were large and completely intact, with corridors and tunnels worming through. The rooms and corridors had become twisted over time, warped by the weight of soil and roots above them, shaped in places by collapse as the world fell into the rooms and the rooms fell into each other.

Meco did not know how many of the Seeds there were; he was certain by now they must outnumber the Blissed. He had seen reset after reset, harvest after harvest, but bereft of memory he could not give voice to his increasing sense of unease.

A line of rooms formed a tunnel, objects both intact and broken filled the floor and corners, stuffed into the cracks in the walls and propped on top of one another like cairns. Objects covering the floor were shattered, little more than splinters that carpeted every room, which felt like pine needles and leaves underfoot. Meco nervously checked his gloves once more, he could not stand the ambush of powerful emotion that contact with his flesh would elicit.

Any object at the top of one of the many cairns, or placed into a crack in the wall, was usually intact, even objects piled up to the ceilings held to this structure. It felt manufactured, deliberate, a curation of reliquaries.

This concentration of thoughts and memories, diffused and scattered, bled into every surface, but it was the dust that floated in the air that provided the weight to the heavy atmosphere – it smelled of wet rotten wood.

The source of the dust was particles of the pollution that infused the objects. Each mote held a remnant of a memory, an atom that was once part of a collective, which had given it cohesion, context and meaning, by now adrift, isolated from its source, no more than a single note of a song, a letter from a story or a feeling or sense whittled down to a thought no deeper than instinct.

This miasma inspired a thrill of panic as Meco approached, it kept the Blissed from exploring the deep places of the sphere, eliciting a pulsating frenzy that ebbed and flowed along the tunnels and rooms with an atmosphere as much mood as memory. These tunnels and rooms had a personality, changeable and erratic, navigation here was only possible by being selective where he placed his gloved hands, for every fragment held a memory of something, a flash of disjointed experience that would dazzle and confuse if touched. More than time was lost in these rooms, here layers of life threaded through the air, brick and soil, every part of these places haunted by desperation and loss, a kaleidoscope of broken lives in constant churn. The atmosphere permeated everyone within and first revealed itself as a bolt of panic, Meco knew and expected this, he steeled his senses, knowledge is a shield and he knew that navigation of chaos was as much mitigation as geography, there would be no complete evasion, no path that would not bring harm to him, but focusing on the chaos could lead to being overwhelmed, a cold radiation of razor-edged thrills entwined with confusion and dread.

Edging deeper into the tunnel through another artificial gap in the walls, Meco pulled out a rusted torch from his back pocket, the light from which he dulled with a cloth. He did this so he could better see any hint of the glow emitted by the Seeds. Not all of them were vocal but all of them shone, burning from the memories they suffered to keep.

Meco emerged into an open space, here tunnels met as a crossing of rooms, connected by a haphazard series of spirals creeping off in all directions like roots. The space and flows of dust had the same presence as a waterfall, it had the same power. Meco struggled to focus at first, there was so many layers of sense and sound. Crouching down, he raised himself onto the balls of his feet, putting the least amount of him in contact with the surface of the tunnel, a practised genuflection. Meco listened intently, he searched through the layers and flows around him looking for the gaps between the overlapping sounds and feelings echoing around him. In decaying orbits his trained subconscious was searching the rags caught on his sharp senses.

The cacophony was radiant, it was both thrilling and mournful, sounds of crying and laughter merged with songs and muttering. Meco knew this was unusual, it meant there were many Seeds hidden away here. Seeds were solitary by nature, when they were in proximity, within sight of one another, it magnified their own anguish, memory called to memory. Misery and manic joy swirled around these tunnels, oil and water mixed by the churn, simultaneously distinct but when in unison were as potent as they were debilitating, it felt like giddy despair and it washed over him, searching for an ingress into his being that practised stoicism refused to provide.

Every Seed on the sphere was grieving for something they cherished and did not want to relinquish, suffering to retain it. But loss was inevitable, it would come either by the erosion of will created by the irresistible pull of the star causing them to surrender, or become reckless in their habits of escape making them easier to hunt down and drag to redemption.

The older Seeds Meco found were particularly dangerous, these Seeds had forgotten the reason they ran from redemption. As with Meco, over time and with proximity to the objects they had gathered, their memories had become corrupted or lost, but core instinct remained fight or flight.

Meco had chosen the Seed he hunted for a reason; the thin man scavenging for solace was lost, his focus was far away and Seeds like this usually did not have much fight in them. The sounds that flowed around him told him there were many more Seeds in these tunnels, and he now had a choice. He could back out and track a new Seed altogether, this was the sensible option, but Meco was loath to delay the harvest, he only needed one more and then his rest could begin. Closing his eyes, he focused on what the tunnels were telling him, drawing the tune from the air like a thread from a tapestry, and let it lead him down.

# Chapter 3 – Between the Swarm and the Feckless Harvest.

Orbiting the star between light and sphere, the engine is the nerve centre of the world. Hourglass shaped, its surface is wire and glass casting prismatic colour on the surface of the sphere above and below, dividing light from life.

At the front of the engine is the operating system of the sphere, known by a single word written on its faded casement – Control.

In the rear of the engine is a ragged, dense collection of tendrils wrapped around central core of metal, this is Robot, it serves the engine.

Robot peered through rheumy lenses at a single monitor that was connected to Control. On this monitor everything on the sphere was recorded and analysed, a harmonisation of precision and logic.

Control was in the midst of a calculation, one that had been repeated 15,721 times so far, searching for a solution, but the system could never be balanced.

Every scenario had been tested; all types of revolutions run. In this process generations had been sacrificed to push the pendulum of change from where it was to its polar opposite at measurable cost, only for it to swing back, never still, an eternal metronome measuring futility.

Control used its programme and the tools it had at its disposal to balance the equation to ensure the sphere survived, but any extreme always brought loss, any compromise infected the crop of Blissed with misery, providing poor quality fuel. The only positive mitigation was when the pendulum of change was in motion.

Misery was the current status of the world, a misery so deep it would take a way of thinking that up until now had been beyond the programming of either occupant of the engine.

Imagination had only recently seeped through the pollution shared by Robot to corrupt Control, this intrusion had mutated into doubt and fear, all of which inspired a conclusion.

Control itself was the system, its habits and patterns were ingrained. The only change potent enough was for that system to remove itself from the world, what followed would be unknown, it would be a leap of faith.

With its tendrils, Robot used the keyboard that surrounded the monitor to flick between endless screens of data and record.

A scene was held on the screen in front of Robot, showing a harvest from ages past, 30,000 cycles ago. There was no earlier information. Control's capacity could only hold that much data before it needed to be overwritten.

The ancient recording showed the sphere little changed from what it now was. Woods and rivers had wandered slightly, paths had been forged, abandoned, and forged again, transient scars on the thick flesh of the world.

Robot continued to click through the data, tapping a tuneless rhythm on the keys and shifting the weight of its frame as it did so. The screech of metal echoed as its supporting tendrils spread wide beneath it and scuttled over the metal and glass frame of the engine.

On the screen was an ancient record where Tij led one of the Blissed by the hand to the golden Blissed field, a highly polished square at the centre of one of the last two towns still inhabited, and here stood 15,000 Blissed, all drawn of their memories, grinning blank vessels, some swaying, some dancing, all grinning in their absence of memory and experience, all taken by Tij to be used as fuel for the harvest.

Robot continued to watch as Tij guided the Blissed to a space at the edge of the square and saw her walk toward the spire, which was a thin, silver jagged shard that extended upward from the corner of the square.

Control flicked the recording forward slightly until Tij reached the base of the spire and sat down on the chair at its base. The recording flicked forward again and showed the spire glow a brilliant white light, this was the sign that the harvest was complete, sufficient memories and experience had been gathered to feed to the star, which edged ever closer, eager for its offering, its meal.

Leaning in closer to the screen, Robot watched intently as the images showed the engine hover over the spire, like a bee above a flower. Here, the harvest was transferred from the spire to the engine in bolts of energy. The light from the silver spire shone brightly as the star neared. The engine ascended moving toward the star at the correct height from the ground and waited.

The distance was optimised by Control as the corona of the star hit the Blissed that stood in the golden field, turning each of them molten, reforming them with new memories and material forged in the star, new elements generated from old, fed back to the Blissed to be worn and lived, so they could use this bright gift to create new memories, forms and knowledge, each one of the Blissed a field freshly sown.

The engine positioned itself as the star opened like the maw of a great beast revealing its writhing inner layers, and at its centre was a core of dull metal. A single spark from the engine struck the core of the star and it returned to life. As the dull metal began to shine bright golden light as it was nourished by a harvest of memories sacrifice by the Blissed. The star then closed its mouth and returned to its place at the centre of the sphere.

In the golden field the Blissed were ablaze with the new memories gifted by the star, all crops must be sown from selected grain of the preceding harvest. Robot watched as the Blissed each became reforged, a new life emerging from the molten flesh, a form, shape and character unlived by them, entirely different from who they were before, a new existence to live, their previous lives now burning as fuel at the core of the star above them.

Robot turned from the monitor as the calculations on the screen paused once again, indicating Control was still lost in hopeless calculation. The harvest came through the engine, it came here to be filtered by Robot.

Scuttling toward its station, Robot moved over the glass and metal of the engine, navigating carefully around the piles of everyday objects that dripped with the pollution that covered everything in a thin oily film, which coated the glass in a dark smear, dampening sound and light.

What the monitor did not show was the part of the process where the harvest coursed through the frame of Robot. Its purpose was to filter out the heavier elements, the memories and emotions that did not burn easily.

Joy was a more reactive element than sadness. The star could burn all, but heavier elements would create less heat and light and the sphere needed a specific amount to survive, to be able to sustain all that lived upon its surface, so the heavier elements were removed.

Everything Robot was consisted of, metal, purpose, and pollution, was a consequence of being the filter for the harvest, purifying the fuel for the star. Over countless times, Robot had begun to think, and dream borrowed thoughts. Robot had sentience, but it was an accretion of unwanted memories, its sentience was split between sadness and purpose.

On either side of the station were two large vats and here was where the heavy elements filtered from the harvest were stored, the pollution of unwanted thoughts, memories, and feelings. The vats had long begun to overflow, Robot could not recall when they didn't. Its programming required it to remove the pollution of the heavy filtered elements but to where?

The heavy elements were once released back into the air like rain, but it had begun to affect the Blissed and the harvest, so this was stopped by Control.

Robot wore its sentience like unwanted, ill-fitting clothes, every thought and alien sensation Robot felt was a consequence of what was cleansed from the harvest. But it was not just the Blissed that were renewed and reset, the sphere itself was cleared of all things created or changed by those that went before. Control did not want the Blissed to be interfered with, philosophies and conspiracies took root-like weeds, and this would affect the harvest, so any history was removed. Control programmed drones that cleaned and maintained the sphere, tending the food supply, the water. These drones only appeared once the world was empty.

Stretching out a tendril to a stack of selected objects, Robot picked out a small picture frame with a painting that had been ripped in half, only the eyes and head remained, it could not see the full face, but the eyes were smiling. Robot had saved many objects from this process of cleansing; its selection was a process driven by a nascent aesthetic that it did not understand but created in its metal frame a fascination.

Taking the picture frame, Robot scuttled over to one of the vats that contained some of the pollution of heavy elements filtered from the preceding harvests, removed the ill-fitting lid, then dipped the frame into the vat. Taking great care to ensure every part of the object was covered, it watched through an aged lens as the eyes of the shredded picture disappeared beneath a layer of dark liquid, then plunged the picture frame deeper into the thick pollution, holding it there for a long minute.

Checking the picture frame was completely saturated, Robot took a moment and brought the object closer to its body, waiting for what the interaction between broken object and pollution would reveal.

Whispers and shadows began to form words that coiled around each other into stories, sparks of light spun into images and the breathing tones of life distilled into music, such creations were easily woven from joy and happiness, but they rang hollow like tin, they were confections not creations. Joy is sweet and burns hot and bright as fuel, but sadness is nourishment, it is what sustains, that which is forged from sadness rings true, it is the bright note of consolation from which solace is built, the ember outlives the flame.

Robot placed the lid back on the vat, the heavy elements absorbed by the picture frame continued to interact with Robot; a truer creation grew from the memory held within the picture frame, images of a sleeping lover here coloured from darker shades of emotion so much sharper than anything born from joy, misery is percussive, felt as well as heard, For a brief moment Robot felt the heartbeat of the owner of this memory, which wires and servos translated into a slow tapping of wire on metal.

There was always a reaction, but they were not always coherent. Robot selected the ones that sang, or whispered tales of a life it had never seen or heard before. The pollution had imbued this picture with a song with a haunting melody. Robot listened to the entire tune, then satisfied, placed it carefully on the floor.

Robot repeated this process, selecting each object from one pile, coating each in turn with the pollution from the vat, and waited, listening to what would be created. Objects whose pollution satisfied Robot's aesthetic were placed on the floor with the picture frame, those that did not were returned to the pile nearest the vat to be reused. All broken things deserved a second chance to become something new.

Satisfied with its selection, Robot gathered up the pile of objects, which included the picture frame, and listened once more. Separately, each object projected its new creation out into the air of the engine. When gathered together they would interact with each other, often this was a cacophony of noise but on occasion it was a chorus, in this instance it was somewhere in between.

Robot's rheumy lens peered through the glass of the engine's surface. Robot knew the orbit of the engine and waited until the appropriate time came around, recognised by the rhythms of implacable ritual orchestrated by Control.

With the curated objects gathered close, Robot pushed a free tendril into the mechanism hidden in the metal that framed the glass of the engine's surface and watched as a door rolled to the side. What was once held tenderly was cast out into the air. Through damaged and time-worn lenses, Robot focused on each of the objects as they fell to the appropriate place, these gifts were once cast across the sphere, but Robot had long since concentrated the sowing to a small section of the world below. Such density of objects would draw the Seeds together, the soil itself would be altered, Robot had observed, different crops needed different soil to thrive, the future was no different.

Some objects smashed into the ground, reduced to splinters, but most did not. The pollution added to the objects' resilience, the density of sadness worked as a shield, if not a parachute.

Someone far below on the surface ran from a dilapidated building at the edge of one of the empty towns that made up the dead, lifeless spaces on the sphere. What did Meco call them? Seeds.

The Seed picked up one of the objects just sown on the surface of the sphere, and Robot watched as the Seed held it close to his head to feel what it contained. He dropped the first two objects but collected the third and fourth before resuming his scavenging. Robot felt a bolt of jealousy crackle along its servos, choice was the greatest gift.

Not all the objects Robot had selected were sown back to the sphere, it still held the picture frame, and it scuttled carefully around the piles of objects back toward the monitor. Robot traced the wires from the back of the screen that connected it with Control as they led through the aperture that separated both parts of the engine, then placed the picture frame and the song it held in the space between them and stopped to listen as the chorus of the objects already there changed slightly, singing stories, and telling songs.

Robot wrapped one of its tendrils around a saturated dog-eared book – this object held the history of all that had passed between Control and Robot – then gently placed the book into the heart of its frame. This would be needed later.

The monitor had begun to flicker rapidly. On the screen was a kaleidoscope of formulae and images, swirls of logic that finally settled on an image of the star. Here the star was analysed and dissected.

The star is a swarm of memories, all flowing in ribbons of light around the core from which they feed. The core is made from the harvest sacrificed by the Blissed and it is from this that the swarm fed. The light and heat that the star emits is created by the collision of this swarm of ribbons, as they consumed greedily, coiling around, and fighting each other over every morsel of memory the harvest offered. The ceaseless collisions of the ribbons flowed past and into one another, only to reform again into new and complex shapes. What drove the frenzy was the preferred meal of the swarm of ribbons – joy, happiness – these meals were the easiest to consume, giving the swarm a rush of energy that caused its light to burn brighter, making it quicker and more potent. Heavier meals only slowed them down and were rejected unless given no choice; the swarm always hunted joy.

Robot saw as the number of the harvest was reduced in the calculation and watched as Control worked toward the unavoidable conclusion. As the amount of the harvest reduced, the star became less stable, its shape changed from the smooth surface of the first calculation to what it was now.

Looking through the glass surface of the engine, Robot saw the star as it was now, the same size as it had been for an age but ribbons of light leapt up like flares before crashing back to its surface, for the swarm that was the star was driven to churn around the core only because of the harvest, the fuel that resided there, which it fed from, and had always been sufficient to hold it together.

Robot listened to the chorus of the objects placed in the aperture between it and Control. They reacted to its frustration and fear, the chords of the music becoming strained, higher in pitch. Control and Filter, both long corrupted by the pollution of heavy elements, now felt the failure of each calculation, what once would have been cold reasoning, a millisecond judgement. A problem to solve now felt like a wound, each refusal to admit defeat cut fresh pain into the essence of their being, it was a borrowed essence, but it was theirs, and they suffered.

Robot pushed a tendril into the gathered coils of his form, reaching inside and pulling from himself an object that he kept within. It was a pen, unremarkable in all ways except that this pen held a story.

Leaning its sensing diodes closer to the aperture toward Control, it listened to the effect the polluted objects Robot had pushed through the aperture had on Control, over time this had changed its very nature. Where once the sound had been the steady predictable metronomic noises of well-oiled machinery, now corrupted by the pollution of heavy elements it had begun to judder and screech, it was a reaction that metal had in common with flesh, and if listened to, told a story of deep suffering. This story had been absorbed by the book that now sat in the heart of Robot.

In the golden field below there stood 5,000 Blissed. This was not enough, Control knows this, there was a critical limit of fuel that was needed to keep the star stable.

Control was running scenarios on the monitor, each scenario a contortion of logic but came to the same conclusion: there was not enough fuel to sustain the star. The projected carnage burnt itself into the lens of Robot and the suffering of Control, a sharp chorus of screaming polluted metal echoed around the engine as Robot gently touched the book that sat at its heart.

# Chapter 4 – Corrupting the Flow of a Greater Thing.

The husk of Enid wore a vacant grin as Tij led her gently by the hand along the path from her home to the town. Enid was gone, the character, the personality had all been taken by Tij; Enid had been given redemption from her agonised life.

The shell that remained was a greedy creature, stripped of one life through redemption it hungered for the new flesh and new material needed for its next existence, one the star will provide once the harvest is complete.

Each new form came with fresh instincts, skills, and abilities, a unique person blended from old material. This transformation would happen quickly and soon the Blissed returned to the sphere, resplendent in their reforged lives, creating new memories and experiences, which will in time also be taken as harvest, a crop re-sown.

Tij looked up at the star, staring with eyes open, forcing its light to sear into her mind. The life she had taken from Enid would be there soon, to be ripped apart and consumed. The lack of peaceful oblivion made it impossible for Tij to grieve.

Within Tij was a struggle, the collection of memories that was her lover began to react to Tij's sadness, her anger. Tij knew these reactions, she expected no less from Enid, her essence was trying to reach out to her, to provide the comfort and solace she did in life, but Enid was just energy now, and any energy when agitated becomes dangerously unstable.

Letting go of the hand of the shell she was guiding, Tij fell to her knees and screamed. Physical pain flowed into her grief like water poured onto molten metal, the resulting explosion of sparks surrounded her like a scorching constellation of anguish, fear, and misery, like useless shattered armour.

There was no one left in the world now, the burden was hers to carry alone. With tears pouring freely down her face, Tij clenched her jaw, mirroring the grin of the shell of her lover that stood before her, utterly disinterested to Tij's suffering.

Seeing the face of the one she loved so lifeless and distant, the balance within Tij shifted from grief to anger. How could she let herself suffer this way, again, like so many times before? Were agony or isolation the only choices in life?

Tij's grief was stubborn, it refused to move on because deep down she felt she deserved to suffer. To feel is to exist but there was enough pain in sorrow itself to flagellate herself with, anger amplified everything and simultaneously added to the weight of loss as it honed its edges.

The reaction from Enid, held deep inside Tij proved one thing at least; she did love her, that one sliver of consolation was the leverage she needed to find her way back to the surface of her misery as grief continued to settle within her like dust, it would form another layer, just one of many.

Tij felt the borders of herself begin to solidify. The lines separating her and the one she loved that she held inside her were drawn, becoming solid, like a scab protecting a wound. Tij felt herself again, she had learnt how to live with what remained once grief subsided. A new shore would be formed from the wreckage of the storm.

Instinctively, Tij reached out a dusty hand to Enid, as if asking for her help to stand up, but the shell just stood grinning, looking right through her.

Putting a hand on the stone of the path, Tij eased herself back to her feet, and looked at the shell in front of her. She did not know exactly what it was like for the people she gave redemption, whether absence was worse than pain. All she knew was that for Tij the absence was much worse.

Placing both her hands at the centre of Enid's back, Tij gently pushed her toward their destination, to the shining Blissed field, the other side of the town. She kept her eyes fixed to the path they had to take; she could not look at Enid without being filled with grief.

Tij steered Enid down the well-trodden path toward the town, which was one of two that sat equidistant along the equator of the sphere; each was identical, although ruination and abandonment had rendered them distinct from one another. The town they moved toward was the last that was inhabited, here the wear and tear was through use and purpose, while everywhere else it was caused by absence and neglect.

The main street was formed on both sides from an escarpment of rooms that pushed up through the surface of the sphere. The Blissed used these rooms as they saw fit, some they used as a home, others as a place of work or play.

Tij guided Enid toward what was once her home and place of work; it was her café, once filled with the noise and chaos of life, its brightly coloured walls and drink-soaked furniture bore the scars of its raucous existence.

It had countless owners over the cycles of harvest, Tij remembered them all. Closing her eyes, she invoked the memory of the sounds and smells of the place when it was full and alive. Tij felt the place inside her, where Enid's essence sat, as it started to shimmer in reaction to this place and the memories it held.

Tij placed a hand on her chest, just below her heart, where Enid was held, and she spoke softly to her.

'The first time I saw you was in this café, at the heart of the swirling laughter and noise, everyone around you was performing, trying to be noticed, to me they were all just ghosts of colour and motion, but you stood out, you were sitting, eyes closed, listening and smiling to yourself.'

Tij appraised the café as she walked through the door, watching the cleaning drones scurrying around busily, erasing the existence of the last harvest. The Blissed were gone, now this was just another empty place, bereft of life but still haunted by it, everyone who once called this home had either sought redemption, or ran from it.

Sitting on a chair next to an overturned table, which was straightened then cleaned by a drone, Tij ran her hand across its wet and disinfected surface and continued to speak to Enid's essence.

'You were sitting on a stool, on its back legs, leaning against a wall, precariously balanced at the heart of a maelstrom of neon and din, I stared at you amazed at the scene, this is a memory I will always treasure, I felt a connection. Your eyes were closed, you were lost in the world and as I walked toward you, I bumped into someone who dropped their drink, he didn't care and walked away, you opened your eyes and smiled, still lost in the flow of a dream hidden from me, you saw me. In that instant the world inverted, the tumult around us became still and solid, you became a blur of colour as you stood, took me by the hand leading me through the chaos, out through the door and into the quieter street. Away from the colour, back to the light. I started to speak, but before I could say a word, we kissed. It was perfect.' Tij scowled as she remembered how it was interrupted: "Please," a voice had called out, "where is she?" Enid's lips had brushed Tij's as they turned toward the pleading voice.

'I remember the man, everything about him, I remember wanting to push him away, anything to force him to leave us alone. But he wouldn't be denied. He pleaded with me: "Redemption, it hurts, please, take the pain away." The man cried then fell to his knees in front of us, I could sense his pain, but I didn't want to take my eyes off you, scared that you would run away. Reluctantly, I pushed you away. Sobbing deeply in front of me was a slim man wearing a torn red shirt and green shorts, his eyes were deep brown, and his dark skin was glowing a dull orange, his face could still be seen, his features were not yet lost in light, not everyone suffered to stay in the world. He was the first of this harvest. It was the beginning of the end, he was the first to seek redemption, I shivered, tense with annoyance by the interruption, and gestured for the man to approach. I remembered the world falling away as the gibbering man came forward. I grasped his hand roughly, feeling the heat emanate from his flesh. I took his memories in an instant, there were so few, his was a short life but to live is to remember and to remember is to endure. In a single bolt he was gone, he once rested where you are now.'

Tij placed her hand back over her stomach. She looked across to the road, long swept clean of life, and nodded toward the spot where it happened. Tij continued: 'There he stood, I gave him redemption, his flesh was dulled and clammy, this man holding my hand was grinning and looking at me with an expression of sated vacancy, an empty vessel, a Blissed. I felt your eyes burning into my back. I was still holding the grinning man's hand, his name was Luke, it was a name that he had only bore briefly, and I dragged him to follow me. I wasn't as angry at his interruption as I was with what it portended – he was the first, the beginning of the end.'

Grief echoes in empty places, and where Tij sat it struck a heavy chord that resonated in her now empty life. Tears fell as she fought away the sadness, loathed to reveal this to the essence of Enid.

Tij continued, telling the story, not just to Enid, but to herself. 'I led him past you who like the others in the street stood there watching, open mouthed, this was something they all knew would happen, but none had yet seen it, it was both new and primal to them, they recognised their own fate in what they witnessed. It was then you ran from behind me, standing between me and the Blissed, you were smiling once again but in that warm smile I saw the shadow of the guileless grin of the Blissed. You threw your arms around me and leant in for a kiss. I had to push you away, I had my purpose to fulfil. You looked so hurt, I had to explain to you that when I gave someone redemption, for a short time I had to carry them with me, at that time it's not just me, there is someone else here. Your smile returned and you squeezed me in a tight embrace, you smelled of cherry liquor and soap, then you said, "I'll wait here for you, when it's just you." It must have been some kiss. I laughed, relieved more than anything despite my nervousness and the fruits of redemption that was washing around inside me. "I'll be here," you repeated.'

Tij looked at the empty form who stood grinning in front of her, she was now standing in exactly the same spot this had happened, but she was gone. Tij felt the glow of the essence inside her become agitated as if it was trying to reach out, to offer comfort, but this time Tij did not respond, and she felt Enid subside.

Looking around the café – anywhere but at the shell in front of her – Tij's gaze dwelt on the obvious and casual detritus of everyday objects, the mess of life all strewn around unlamented. Another pulse of grief struck Tij, here was where our life together began, her eyes fell onto empty glasses, overturned chairs, books scattered on tables, all were simple monuments to a life lived, each object unremarkable in their time but rendered by absence and loss into precious relics.

The drones continued to clean the sphere, a harvest of their own. It was something Tij often sat and observed. It occurred to Tij that they had the same job, both versions were a redemption of sorts, another form of recycling, it was a continual process of the erasure of unique things, the difference was that what Tij took was visceral, people are shaped through use and habit, just as much as any object, in this they are the same.

A life was a collection of things as much as memories, an object can pin you absolutely to a precious moment, it retained the marks of use that could not exist any other way than how it was worn and used by a particular person, in a particular way. The real sense of them – scent on a shirt, lipstick on a cup, the bent pages of their favourite book – are irrefutable, unique, and sacred.

All was being swept away, piece by precious piece, all recycled, purged of its character, and returned in another form.

Tij turned once more to Enid who was still staring forward, grinning at nothing. Looking up Tij could see past the edges of the star, and along the road the reflections of the other Blissed field, with the spire at its edge, though this one had dulled over time becoming overgrown and tarnished, the other field was still visible and Tij knew exactly where to find it, just another ruined place, another sign that the sphere was not what it was.

Looking forward, Tij could see where her destination lay in front of her, this Blissed field was impeccably maintained shining bright gold, the silver spire looming beyond beckoning her toward it. Almost there. Placing her hands firmly on Enid's back, Tij gently urged Enid's shell toward it.

The Blissed field they headed toward shone through care and use; it amplified the light of the star above in its slightly concave form. All the Blissed she had given redemption to were here gathered all over the field. Some were standing, others sat or sprawled.

The air itself seemed golden, strewn with dust and motes. The light here was diffused by the reflected surface into a mist-like haze, each mote a prism. At its edge was the spire, the machine Tij would use to send the redeemed, the harvest, to await collection by the engine.

Grinning or laughing, all the motions of the Blissed were languid, slowed as they revelled in absence, all staring upward in adoration, their arms raised high reaching up to the star, and the new life that was promised. Tij remembered thinking this was beautiful, once. There were thousands here and she had taken from each one of them the harvest of their short lives.

Tij had in her time redeemed the people closest to her, people she cared for, she had brought them to this very place, seeing the shells of them grinning back at her. She was the means of their escape, an escape from the world and from her. Tij saved her own keepsakes at home, worn and shattered as they were, she was a lover of broken things.

All the Blissed here had wanted this, they had sought redemption joyously, and eagerly they considered it a natural conclusion, an end of a chapter of a book enjoyed but only ever read once. Enjoyed yes, but rarely understood.

The Blissed field was the waiting place, its reflective surface offered the merest taste of what was in store once the reset commenced. Echoes of light would sweep through the Blissed; in this field they rested, haunted by the things they did not have, craving the new forms and lives the star would give them in return for their sacrifice that they would soon imbibe.

This proximity to the star and its influence made the Blissed malleable. To ensure a useful harvest of memories in future they would not only be renewed they would be reborn, reshaped. Their primal core remained, a knot of selfish instinct that always drove the Blissed to feed on light, only becoming sated when they drew a new life and form from what they consumed, like a mosquito drawing blood. Control had tried at various times to manipulate this instinct, but all attempts met with nothing other than horrifying consequences.

The primal core was a sliver of razor-sharp obsidian that would shred on contact anything that brushed against it, but it was easy to circumvent or sink into soft sand and render vestigial.

Renewal would see the Blissed shaped into new forms, it could be as simple as a new face, a new height, someone once beautiful now plain, limbs removed or senses taken or altered, behavioural or mental acuity would soar or sink, magnified, or constrained, gender, sexuality, everything would shift. It was a coerced freedom, but it was exhilarating.

There was no established pattern as to who would become what, it was completely random and into these new forged forms would flow the recycled memories direct from the star.

Tij guided Enid to an empty space on the Blissed field and she waited to see if Enid would look back, giving any indication of remembrance, but she knew it was hopeless, Enid remained completely still, staring up at the star. Tij folded her anger deep down into herself, somewhere adjacent to where the essence that was Enid resided temporarily. She had the sudden notion of cages, one containing the ghost of a precious life, the other the part of herself she had to restrain. Redemption was a box; she did not know if it was finite.

Looking up through tear-filled eyes, she could see the eternally hungry star and the world that surrounded it, tendrils of rivers and streets, towns and forests reached around, underneath, overhead and behind the star, all the paths of life were entrapped in orbit.

Each time Tij redeemed someone she distilled the character of the person within her. She wondered how much of Enid would go as fuel and what parts of her would be filtered by the engine, weighing joy and sadness. The thought left her cold, but Tij would never know what parts of their life together the engine would see as fit to burn.

However much the star needed fuel and the sphere needed the star, Enid was worth so much more to Tij than a season of nourishing light, feeding the trees and crops, to be danced in by the next generation.

If Tij could only keep Enid, a single person to love, did her devotion, her sacrifice not deserve that? There was no one to ask, Tij's duty and fate were concrete, she knew the engine ran things, but she would never know how, its mechanisms and processes were alien and distant.

Leaving the Blissed fields behind her Tij felt relief, the only thing more difficult than leaving Enid behind, the shell that was Enid, was seeing her there, the eyes, the face, all the same as before but empty, the spark had left Enid. The essence of her was now in Tij and it had been reacting, becoming unsettled by the proximity to her former life, to the pain her passing was causing, it was the last thing they would have in common.

The field itself held a sense of threat mixed with impermanence, which repelled her to the core. It was an alien environment, like being underwater where the pressure surrounded her, compelling her to exhale precious breath, every step she took from that place felt like an escape.

Moving to the edge of the Blissed field Tij did not turn, as she moved away, she felt the essence that was Enid inside her change from frenzied iridescence and reducing slowly to a glow. In this calmer state, Tij felt able to send all that remained of the one she loved to the engine, though with all her heart she did not want to.

# Chapter 5 – Seeds and Soil.

Meco used his teeth to cut off the final layer of tape that ran across the gap between his glove and sleeve, then padded the thick, black cotton overalls, checking the tape over his bootlaces, and breathed a sigh, the taste of adhesive filled his mouth.

Leading away from him was a hole broken through a painted wall, which led to a tunnel beyond formed by warped door and window frames that had been tortured into haphazard shapes by subsidence. Meco placed a gloved hand on the wall, resting his head against it, straining to see into the rare dark of the tunnel. He could see the stratification of crooked broken rooms made of brick and stone.

Meco hid his bag of tools safely under some rubble and stood flexing his gloved hands. He drew a deep breath of light fused air and cautiously stepped forward into the tunnel.

His boots crunched on the compacted floor, which consisted of soil, rubble and the splinters of many broken objects that had been dropped by the Seeds.

Turning his head to one side, Meco listened intently to the chorus in the tunnel as he reached for the torch that rested in one of his many deep pockets. He flicked the switch off and on in quick succession, neither light or shadow consoled him, it was the power he had to change between these two states of existence that steadied his nerves. Finally, he turned the torch off placing it back into a deep pocket as his senses adjusted to the darkness.

The tunnel ahead glowed weakly; it was faint light reflected in the compact walls glistening with moisture and splintered objects. The first sound that caught his attention was the high, thin note of a woman crying.

This sound was not emitted from the Seed he was hunting. The scars on his body reminded him that Seeds were unpredictable and occasionally lethal, any disruption to their symbiosis with the objects they had collected, any hint of danger to the cocoons they had woven for themselves from the stories and songs, would meet with an attack born of absolute desperation. Meco's every instinct led him to avoid confrontation with any of the Seeds, unless absolutely necessary. He had chosen his prey carefully, and he would stalk it patiently with care and precision.

Sweat began to drip down Meco's back as he crept deeper into the tunnel. A solid heavy dread amplified this moment to bring a rush of adrenaline causing the damp hairs on his neck to stand up. His instinct was a skittish thing, when tempered by finesse, caution, and precision it was an ally, but a skittish one nevertheless; even a trained subconscious is a beast of burden, but it could still kick and trample him if given a chance.

Meco pressed on further, as the tunnel began to get steeper, he placed his hand on the splinter-choked rubble walls. Wincing suddenly as a small shard of glass stabbed through the thick gloves, the shock was more than pain, every splinter, every object down here was drenched in heavy emotion and memories he wanted to avoid.

He pulled the glass from his glove, closing his eyes as a sense of alien grief washed over him, in its wake was a few intelligible whispered words, and it was gone. Annoyed, Meco threw the small glass splinter to the floor and stamped it into dust.

The layers of rooms and rock that made up the tunnel were a convergence of deep time, but the compaction of the ground beneath him, caused by the generations of feet that must have passed over this ground, was covered in fresh tracks.

A chorus of voices echoed down the tunnel, echoing on the warped windows and doors set askew in the walls, which formed a junction, each frame led into other tunnels, snaking away in every direction.

Meco could pick out certain sounds like grabbing loose threads in the air. There was manic laughter, high in tone but rasping, interspersed with sharp annoyed whispering and someone calling out a name repeatedly. It was overwhelming at first, he struggled to focus on any single layer of sound, as the cacophony shifted endlessly into new forms. A wave of sound surrounded him, it began to react to his emotions, the air resonated with the taught, heavy atmosphere of this place. It was reacting to his presence, his confusion and frustration, the sounds and images were starting to coalesce, almost making sense, and then they were gone.

Switching the torch on Meco continued down the glistening tunnel, careful to avoid unnecessary contact with the walls. Meco squinted as he peered toward the glow emanating from the tunnel, which sloped downward in uneven compacted steps. The glow increased into a low light and Meco could almost see clearly. It was at this moment where experience and instinct sat in balance. Judging by the red light that crept along the wall of the next corner, there was a Seed. Meco edged closer, he started to hear the tell-tale sounds of the Seeds who often talked to themselves, usually playing all the roles in the conversations split by random utterances of nonsense and emotional outbursts, all interspersed with sudden crying, screaming and laughter.

An indicator of how the Seed may react was how brightly it glowed. This showed the age of the Seed. Holding onto memory, especially approaching a harvest, caused the Seed to glow. Enduring countless harvests caused the Seed to burn red or orange – the brighter the shade the deeper the agony.

Meco sought the Seeds whose inexperience drove them to gather objects hurriedly, without discernment, desperate as they were to build a solace from what they had collected to hide from the pain caused by the memories they refused to surrender.

Opportunity now aligned with need, as much as Meco wanted the hunt over, he could not rush, patience was his most reliable weapon.

As Meco tentatively approached the corner, the broken tune of the Seed that was his prey drifted from the tunnel beyond,

Meco felt the ground shake beneath his feet as the sound of the Seed was lost in the dull clatter of collapsing brick and soil.

Meco covered his mouth and quickly turned to the wall to shield himself. Closing his eyes tightly, he held his breath as the dust cloud swirled around him. The dust was filled with more than debris, it was laced with shining mica, the crushed remains of countless shattered objects, each retaining a fraction of faded memory. Each speck of mica that landed on uncovered skin was a pin prick injecting alien emotion into him, the pain was nothing, it was the potent random sensations that he dreaded.

Deep sorrowful moans filled the air. Meco quickly peered around the corner, through the mica strewn air, his fingers reached for the torch in his pocket, flicking the switch off and on, as he identified the cause. Part of the tunnel roof had collapsed, and the cocoons of two Seeds had dropped and lay broken on the ground in sections no bigger than a small door. The moans were being uttered by the two Seeds, both glowed a bright, deep-red. Meco knew the brighter and deeper the light the greater the agony caused by whatever memory they suffered to hold on to. Without the solace of their crafted cocoons, carefully built from curated objects, their pain was intensified.

Meco watched as the Seeds scrambled in the dirt, desperate to regather the broken sections, tuning out their cries as he listened for the song of his prey, which was disappearing ahead.

He could return to the surface, wait for another opportunity, but his need for the harvest to end was too strong. The Seeds began to hit each other with burning limbs, fighting over a piece of solace.

Timing his opportunity, running around the corner, he pressed himself onto the wall of the tunnel as the Seeds rolled on the floor. He was almost through when he heard the crack of glass beneath his boot. He didn't even have time to turn as a scorching arm reached around from behind him, lifting him in the air. He could feel the heat stabbing through his thick overalls as he saw the second Seed stand and launch itself back into the fight.

Meco was thrown across the tunnel, landing in the heart of the rendered cocoon that was solace to one of the Seeds.

A flicker book of memories coursed through Meco, his every sense overwhelmed with the assault, everything was loud, static-filled with every shade and colour, he was lost, there was no ground, no air only light and sensation, then the first memory of the flicker book snapped into focus.

Meco felt emersed in clear cold water, any pain he felt from the impact was gone, this was not his body. He looked at his form; he was a naked woman, twisting through the water gracefully. Meco felt the physical difference first; a right hand was missing, and the cool water electrified along nerves, this body at this moment felt free and alive. The emotional difference was stark, the lightness of being, the dizzyingly alien sense of joy, there was no crushing weight of purpose or anger, which was the foundation of Meco's form.

Bursting through the water to the air above, the dark long hair of Meco's new form spread across the surface. All sensations and feelings were potent and visceral. Meco felt everything as if he himself was swimming, but he was not in control, none of the movements were his, everything was predetermined, this was a memory.

A short, dark-haired man with strong arms, sun-kissed skin and a close-cropped beard was wading from the bank of the river as a playful grin crept across his face. The rush of attraction sent shivers through Meco, his borrowed flesh now covered in goosebumps, aching to be touched. Dipping under the gentle waves of the lake, Meco looked up to the star. The pure yellow light poured through the water in sunbeams; this woman loved the star she served and the life it had given her. Meco was repulsed and jealous of this joyful moment.

The scene flicked over – Now Meco was surrounded by a crowd of people dancing to frenetic rhythms that coiled through the air. Meco felt the bass pound his gyrating new body. The smell of fresh sweat and incense filled the air with the clamour of people singing along to the words of a song the body knew but Meco did not.

Dark fireworks exploded overhead, stark against the bright-yellow star above. Meco felt pleasure wash through the dancing body as the fireworks formed into cascading silhouettes of flowers. The crowd cheered, Meco was grabbed by those around him, spinning him round in a communal embrace. He was drunk and fell on the floor, the group collapsed on top of him, laughing. He felt part of the world like never before; he loved everyone around him slowly getting to their feet, all clothing was red and orange, covered in splashes of coloured powder and stained with spilt food and drink.

Meco knew this was one of the many festivals thrown by the Blissed in honour of the star. He had seen them before, but he did not remember being part of one.

Before sadness could take root in Meco the scene changed once again. Now he was running through a forest familiar to Meco. This body was fit and strong and its experience of the forest Meco knew was very different. Meco knew every tree and dip, he knew the world as a butcher knows a carcass.

This body was sprinting barefoot through a meadowed glade, heart racing, the sound of wind through the trees brought a cleansing sense of elation, a flock of starlings murmured overhead, a bee buzzed closely past his face.

To this form, the forest was filled with music and sensation, it felt part of the sphere that wrapped the star, something beyond duty, it was devotion.

The next image was met with silence. Meco realised this new form was deaf and hidden under a quilt, lying on his front in a deep comfortable bed. The body shook with laughter as his lover kissed his way up his calves. He felt the brush of lips across the length of his thigh, briefly across his buttock to his lower back, which arched as his very essence was filled with desire.

The lover gently pushed himself inside, as he kissed the back of this body's neck, now lost in a maelstrom of lust and yearning.

Then Meco was in the main street of the half-empty town. The emotion here was in shocking contrast. Anger he recognised, but it was honed by desperation, grief, and helplessness. The body he was in was being held down to the ground. Meco could taste blood on his lips and his body was covered in stinging bruises as he was held firmly.

He looked up and called out to a woman who was glowing a dull orange and walking slowly away from him. He called out again: 'Sarah!' She neither stopped nor turned, but continued to walk toward a figure that Meco knew all too well, this was Tij, and Sarah was begging her for redemption.

One of the Blissed holding him down was whispering into his ear: 'This is the price, this is our life, let her go.'

The body replied: 'Don't leave me, please don't ... no, no ...' the last few words were lost in sobbing as the body watched the glow disappear from his lover's form, free of all memory. Tij took Sarah by the hand, turning her toward the Blissed field. Meco felt the heart of the body sink and shatter, wracked by loss that intensified when he saw the grinning form of his vacant lover, as Tij led her past.

The three Blissed holding him down released him. He stood, turned to them, and spat on the floor as he took the path out and away from the town. The body looked up at the star and Meco at last felt empathy as the body was filled with hate.

In that moment, Meco knew what solace was, it isn't a state of being, a memory or consolation, it is a person, someone cherished and irreplaceable. The Seeds built their cocoons dedicated to the memory of someone they'd lost, replacing what time and pain wears away with a poultice cobbled together from borrowed memories salvaged from the pollution-soaked objects they collect from the dreaded starlit world above.

These imperfect cocoons are brittle shields protecting the Seeds from some of the burning agony, which is the price they choose to pay to keep the memories of the ones they love alive and not surrender them to the siren call of the star. Before the flicker book could restart, Meco felt the touch of scorching hands and the familiar sensation of being lifted in the air.

One of the burning Seeds threw him away from the ruin of its solace and rushed forward, hammering into Meco and barrelling him over the edge of the crumbling ledge. Meco fell through the air, smashing through layers of cocoons, each impact throwing debris and dreams into constellations of dust in the broken tunnel. The inhabitants were brightly lit smears, screaming music of fear and hate.

Every sense was reeling, the world was a mix of brightly coloured oil and flame, the desperate fury of the Seeds struck into Meco, every strike sent waves of pain through his body, where they overlapped inside him it felt like his flesh was being sliced open.

Seeds dropped through the layers above him as the brittle ground continued to collapse. The pain helped Meco focus, becoming a point of gravity where his consciousness could gather itself. As the fallen Seeds continued to strike and gouge at Meco, the greater the agony they inflicted the more he felt like himself.

Dodging between lunges and the relentless attacks, he knew the Seed, lost in its own pain, would keep attacking him until he managed to escape. Looking around, he saw what was left of a narrow layer of brick leading to a Seed-free area of the tunnel, and he scrambled across it hurriedly.

Below him he could see a chasm, an open wound between strata of brick, soil, and countless Seeds. Here the tunnels had collapsed into each other, yawning like an open wound. He jumped the last distance, and turned to see if he was followed, but the Seed had returned to rebuilding its solace, crawling on its hands and knees, searching through the rubble.

Meco's breach through the ceiling of the tunnel was just one of many collapses. He could see this underground world cracked open like a geode beneath him; everything glittered in shades of red and orange, diffused by air thick with dreaming dust.

All light in the deep places of the sphere is emitted by the burning Seeds, the source was the same, but the shade varied, where solace was most brittle, incomplete, or broken the Seeds burnt bright red in their agony, changing to orange when the cocoons were solid and stable, pain mitigated by the solace, but there was no true escape from pain.

He watched as the dust fell around him, wiping the stinging grime and sweat away with the back of his glove, and for a moment lost himself in the refracted chorus of sound and light. His reverie was interrupted as a thin song wormed its way through the dense air behind him, the sound of his prey.

In this deep place, burning people crafted unwanted and unloved emotions into inspiration and solace, woven into cocoons by the Seeds from curated objects drenched with heavy memory. All gathered from the same part of the sphere above, for many cycles this was a successful hunting ground for Meco, the rhythms, sensations and texture of this place was known, if not kind, to him, this familiarity provided a scrap of solace, now this had been lost.

Leaving the frenzy of the chasm behind, Meco sighed deeply as he cautiously crept away along another branch of tunnel, carefully avoiding touching the wall, and listening intently to every slight crack emanating from the brick and soil around him.

The anguished moans of desperate Seeds followed him down the tunnel becoming gradually weaker with each careful step and easier for Meco to tune out.

The density of Seeds was much lower toward the edges of the tunnel, the greatest safety was at the greatest depth, and this was where the oldest and most dangerous of the Seeds resided. Meco had long since harvested the low hanging fruit, it was curious how his prey had gotten so far on this occasion, he mused that the tunnels stood firm for his prey, only collapsing when he drew near. Meco laughed briefly to himself, he shook his head and breathed deep breaths, his heart still raced. His attempt to gather himself was interrupted by the song of the Seed ringing clear and true; the air in this part of the tunnel was not choked with dust and every one of his senses felt sharper.

The tunnel began to slope upward and a breath of fresh air brushed Meco's cheek, another entrance to the tunnels must have opened up in the surface of the sphere, another change for him to understand. The voice of the Seed bounced its way along the tunnel in front of him, growing with every step, luring him forward.

Meco wanted this to be over, his total and absolute exhaustion left him hollow, all he had was fatigue and purpose, not every scar was obvious. He shivered slightly in the freshening air, he just wanted respite from the world, one more Seed and the harvest would be complete. He brushed the nascent tear away, irritated.

Angry with himself, Meco's pace began to quicken, faster and faster he put his racing heart to use, the thin scattering of cocoons became a blur as his senses locked onto the song of the Seed. He felt sweat trickle down his back as his chest heaved deep breaths. The song was steps away. He careered recklessly around a curve in the wall and smashed into his prey.

This hunt had left its mark on Meco, and he would return the favour. The Seed burning bright orange was now silent, winded by the impact, and was struggling to get to his feet, the objects he had carefully collected lay scattered on the floor around him.

Meco wanted the fight, he was ready for someone else to suffer, he ran across and kicked the Seed in the stomach, as he rolled over, he stamped down repeatedly. The Seed desperately reached out to one of the objects he had dropped – it was a small book, which Meco kicked away down the tunnel.

Meco swept away any object the Seed reached out for.

'Get up,' he screamed into the Seed's face. Meco couldn't see its features but could hear the Seed speak.

'Let me go, it hurts so much, please, please,' it gasped, as it fought for breath. The Seed was trying to crawl away.

'Why does it hurt?' Meco snarled, grabbing the Seed's hair. 'Tell me why it hurts.'

'He left me, all we had, he left me here, I can't lose him again.'

Meco let go of his hair and watched as the Seed continued to crawl through the dust of the tunnel floor.

He knew what the Seed would say, it was what they all said in one way or another. Meco had seen the Seeds fight for what they loved but watching how this one, weak with a grief that was so obviously fresh and raw, suffering against the inevitable, stunned Meco for a second.

His anger fell away. All the agony this Seed endured was to keep the memory of someone alive in spite of the siren call of the star and its promise of joy and renewal, this Seed wanted the life it had, it didn't want to change.

'I understand,' Meco whispered to the Seed, 'but I need my rest, the life you had will burn in the star and the Blissed you will become will dance in its light and warmth.'

The Seed was not trying to escape, it was seeking the solace he had started to build, it was no more than half-complete, but it was intricately wrought, dense with pollution-soaked objects all chosen to make the Seed able to endure. Meco walked over to the cocoon and stamped it into splinters, once more he was the butcher of solace. The hollow cry of the Seed told him his prey was broken.

Leaning heavily on the wall, Meco allowed the alien memories mitigate his rising guilt. This was his purpose, this was what he was for, to ensure the harvest is completed, and purpose was all he had in the world.

Meco held out his hand toward the Seed, who was lying in a foetal position, sobbing deeply, the dust was wet with tears and blood.

'Come on, let's put an end to this, come on.' Meco gently lifted the burning Seed to its feet and held it until it was steady and could stand.

The colour of the Seed had started to change in accordance with its suffering, once orange it was now a dull red, its whole posture changed, it was bending slightly forward, head pointed down, defeated.

The Seed turned to look at Meco who stepped away, placing himself between any possible escape down the deeper parts of the tunnel. The Seed's suffering would do Meco's work for him now, there was no way out, no solace could be built, there was no escape. It held out its hand to Meco, there was no one else to help it toward unwanted redemption. Meco took the Seed's hand tightly, letting the heat burn his flesh, and led him back to the surface.

# Chapter 6 – Spire.

A silver spire loomed above Tij, broad at the base, becoming thinner as it reached up toward the star high above. Embedded into its surface were twisting cords of copper in whirling patterns, symmetrical at first, becoming smaller, intricate, and more random like sprawling vines as they reached upward to its apex. The copper pattern ended in three strong cords coiled around a perfectly flat, black metal disc.

At the base of the spire, set into its very structure, was a tall chair, wrought from the same copper and silver. The chair was simultaneously burnished by time and polished through use. Metal threads twisted into tight, ever decreasing spirals, forming an outline of someone sitting.

Tij was lost in thought, staring at the spire, with one hand covering the place just below her heart where the essence of Enid sat. She could hear Meco and his prey approaching. The sobbing of the Seed heralded their arrival.

Glancing sideways, she could see the dark-red glowing form draw near and watched as it fell to its knees when it saw her, still sobbing, utterly defeated. Meco was breathing heavily as he tore the tape around his gloves with his teeth, steam of effort emanated from him, his clothes were drenched in sweat and blood. He was avoiding Tij's gaze. He ripped the last of the tape away, throwing it aside, and then proceeded to smack the dust from his black overalls with the gloves, visibly wincing as he did so.

Looking across at Meco, who now wore a scowl as he stared up at the spire that loomed above, she could see that he was bleeding, he was also muttering to himself under his breath. He was old, he always had been, but every harvest had taken its toll, each carved into his very flesh. Meco's entire body told the story, in this they were the same, but her scars could not be seen. The star always healed if given time, but there was no part of his flesh not covered by scars. She wondered if they were all layered down to the very core of him. Meco, like Tij, had been shaped by time into forms useful to the service of the sphere.

Meco was truly a horrific sight, but his wounds, though healing, were worse than usual; he looked distraught. At his side the Seed was staring directly at her. Tij would be the end of him, it would be a release from his pain, an unwanted gift, and Tij could feel its enmity toward her.

Beaten and broken, though Tij knew Meco didn't need to use force to compel the Seeds, most were rendered malleable through their own agony. He never failed to succeed in hunting the elusive toward redemption. Meco's scowl slipped just for a moment into a look of desperation and what looked like a tear rolled down his cheek. He saw she was watching him and stared back, Tij couldn't read what he was thinking.

The Seed at his side tried to stumble back to its feet when Meco covered the short distance between them in less than a second, grabbed its head in both his hands and forced the Seed to look upward at the star.

'Don't,' Tij whispered as she walked toward them. Meco released the Seed, muttering something under his breath as he stepped back. She could hear the Seed sobbing between deep breaths, its posture had changed, no longer stiff, and poised like a cornered beast but limp in defeat, the last thread of resistance had left its body.

Meco stared intently at Tij and opened his mouth to speak. Seconds passed in silence. He frowned, shaking his head as he took a few steps past her and sat heavily and clumsily on the floor, curling up into a ball, and turned away from Tij.

The Seed's gaze was locked on the star, its flesh radiated a deep-red light that Tij read like a book. From its colour and shade, she discerned something of the life the Seed had lived. She knew what each pulse and shade meant; she knew the type of memory the Seed had held onto.

The ingredients were the same, a blend of grief, anger, sadness or fear, the loss of someone else or the loss of themselves, or losing a life they had cherished, whatever it was they suffered terribly to keep. Standing in front of the Seed, Tij stroked her hand across its cheek, rubbing the sweat and blood between her fingers, gritting her teeth in irritation as she flicked her gaze toward Meco, who was still lying on the floor. The Seed burnt in the colour of grief.

Tij felt a glimmer of empathy, but it was fleeting, replaced by a flash of resentment. The thought of adding the alien grief of this Seed to her own, to take this Seed's memories inside her and have them stir in the same place with what was left of Enid, made Enid's final journey less personal, but she could not deny the harvest, there was no such thing as choice.

She listened to the familiar sound of tears sizzling on burning skin. The Seed's features were lost in light, covered in blood, it was oblivious to the world and was gibbering frenetically through cracked hands that covered its face.

Tij continued to read the light that pulsed from the Seed as well as listening intently to everything uttered. It wasn't here by choice; it was a fate it struggled hard to avoid. Redemption was not a gift this Seed wanted, and its shade radiated anger, this was not a dutiful sacrifice, it was theft.

Like Enid, this Seed did not want to surrender the life it had fought and suffered for so long to keep. This Seed chose to burn, to remember even if it hurt, and Tij loved him for that.

Placing her hands gently on the Seed's shoulders, Tij was now face to face with the burning Seed, the heat pouring from it hit her in waves, thick calloused skin protected her hands from the worst, her hands burnt with pain but did not blister.

She closed her eyes, reached out through her hands for a connection through burning flesh, searching for the essence of the Seed.

Every essence varied, this one was cold, bright, and small and it held every memory the Seed had treasured, in a quick sharp second Tij snatched it all away.

Arching her back in shock as the cold heavy essence settled inside her, Tij focused, steering the new essence away from Enid, she did not want any of this Seed's memories corrupting her lover. With practised ease, Tij kept Enid with her for a few moments longer.

The heat from the Seed was gone, its shoulders no longer shook from sobbing, it was perfectly still. Tij could feel its shallow breathing on her face.

Opening her eyes, Tij saw the grinning Seed in front of her. She recognised this Seed, she knew every Blissed on the sphere, and deep in her memory she could recall every form they had ever taken. His name had been Kai, he was young, they were all young, he had been a musician, he played the piano beautifully and she remembered he adored Kulbir, who was among the last hundred Tij had redeemed.

Tij had to remember, of course, this is how redemption worked after all; for someone to be forgiven a life it must always be remembered, redemption was the transition from who they were to what they are now, from life to memory, and Tij was the conduit, she was the very end for all, both the willing Blissed and the desperate Seeds. All had either sought her or had been dragged through the soil of the sphere by Meco. Redemption was inevitable, the sphere must be able to move forward, its existence must be ensured, the harvest must be fulfilled at any cost.

Tij owed each one that had come to her a place in her eternal memory; it was a poor epitaph, but it was all she could offer. Every scrap of evidence of life from the sphere would be removed, she must remember every life, she was redemption.

Each life taken from the Seeds by Tij in this place would be fuel for the world. It was the taking of all the visceral and abstract things that each contained, each life was unique in structure but common in element, and all were destined to be converted into fuel for the star to burn, to light and heat the world, a world that was now empty, a fallow field to be re-sown.

Tij glanced at Meco, who was still lying on the floor. There was nothing she could say to him; it was not that she lacked the words, but it had all been said before, every word, every cadence, uttered countless times, there was no consolation for the two eternal servants of the sphere.

Once a brave Seed, Kai was returned to the comfortable absence of the Blissed. Taking him by the hand, Tij urged him to complete his journey to the Blissed field. Kai's long blond hair clung to his damp neck, wet with sweat. Tij could see the gentle blue eyes and remembered his easy smile, that last time they met he had made her laugh, he was charming and funny and all that was left was a grinning shell, skin smeared with dirt and blood.

Tij could see the damage his struggle with Meco had wrought upon his flesh – a broken nose and split lip had been bleeding profusely, quickly healing under the light of the star. It was just another erasure of a life well-lived and fought for. Just another one of the Blissed, Kai, was an empty vessel. Tij found him difficult to look at, an image of Enid grinning at her flashed across her mind. Tij fought back tears as she felt Enid's essence start to stir in response, and then slowly settle as Tij regained control.

A hollow being stood before her. It should have been a comfort to Tij that along with the memories she had taken, the life she ended, she had also removed all the suffering, all the pain, but to Tij it was no consolation at all.

The edge of the Blissed field was mercifully close, and like she had done with Enid, she guided the empty shell to its place in the field, among the rest of the harvest. As she released his hand she could see Enid, standing where she had left her. She was smiling an unfamiliar smile, her eyes fixed on the star. Tij felt her heart drop as the empty husk of Enid began to slowly sway and spin, raising her arms, lifting them above her head, she was dancing, basking in the light that was fuelled from the memories of the previous harvest.

Tij took a hesitant step toward her lover, she wanted to hold her one last time, but what was dancing in the shining Blissed field was hollow, a living ghost waiting for the gift of a new life and form to be bestowed by the ravenous star. Tij let her grief spill over, filling her, letting it wash around both the essences inside her, the one that was cold barely noticed, Enid stirred, agitated, causing a heat to build up that fizzed and crackled inside her. Tij let her lover suffer for a long moment, revelling in the pyrrhic consolation.

The harvest was fulfilled, enough memories harvested, Tij's duty drove her back the short distance toward the spire on the edge of the Blissed field, filled with the empty remnants of a life.

Turning toward the spire, Tij traced the shape of it from its base to its very tip with her finger as the engine moved from its path in orbit around the star to its place overhead, inching toward the disc atop the spire where it hovered, waiting for delivery of the harvest.

The spire was the silo for the harvest. The memories of the Blissed who had been given redemption were stored here like grain. It would be taken by the engine in its entirety and fed to the star once filtered. To do otherwise would mean the star would dim and brighten in accordance with the regularity of the fuel sent; such a method was not acceptable to Control.

The star would not have seasons, its light would not ebb, the sphere is optimised based on a certain level of light, the Blissed were just another crop. The animals, everything, owed its existence to the star as it was, in its eternal state, and the harvest made this possible.

With the Blissed field now behind her Tij looked straight at the star. Closing her eyes, she could feel its light begin to creep its way beneath her closed lids. She looked aside, everyone she had ever loved had been consumed to create this light that nourished the beauty of the verdant sphere around her.

Tij began the short journey to the spire, Meco still lay on the floor, completely still. She almost walked straight past; she was filled with her own grief. She stood over him and looked down, both his scarred hands covered his face, his noisy breathing bubbled between his fingers.

Life is light and grief is its shadow, one in which we all have stood and will stand again, yet there are so few words to describe it, or console those who suffer, reused, respoken words, spat out like over-chewed food into tear-streaked faces.

Tij did not offer anything new, she sang an old song with its all-too-familiar melody woven from every word that had already been said — and they flowed effortlessly from her lips, a litany of consolation spoken in the deep cadence of sincerity. It wasn't a lie but there was no feeling behind it, the song was overplayed and had lost its impact, but it was all there was. She projected each word at Meco, but he knew it wasn't for him, it was for herself, grief is selfish, this he knew.

Meco rolled onto his front and grunted as he struggled to his feet, still refusing to meet Tij's gaze. He would follow her to the spire, he always did.

The walk to the spire would take moments. The ground of the Blissed field was a bright mirror, reflecting the star, it gave the impression that everyone was floating in light.

The great spire of the machine loomed large as Tij approached its base. She held the last of the harvest she had within her; it was a struggle to keep calm, but exhaustion had begun to take hold. She felt its dull numbness surround her like a cloak, she just wanted it all to be over.

Tij knew that grief was an amputation, she had to continue as if nothing had changed, all for the peace and comfort of others, of the essences she carried inside her. In the secret corners of her heart Tij wanted to let the pain loose, to feel its full effect, to let herself suffer and feel, to use grief itself as a punishment for her existence, her purpose. If each loss was an amputation, what was left of her after all this time? At what point can nothing else be taken? Was there ever such a state, a singularity where the line was drawn, here and no further?

Looking at the star above Tij felt nothing but guilt at its light, every memory that was burning up there she had taken from one of the Blissed and carried inside her, it was the light that fed the world, the trees, crops, and grass, which in turn fed all life. To Tij, light was an accumulation of everyone she had lost, the star was entirely made from history, taken and reworked. Was there any recollection of Tij, any knowledge of the lives she had felt? The selfish part of Tij, the part where grief always roots itself, needed this to be true.

Enid was responding to her despair, as in life she wanted to come to Tij's aid, to stand with her and ease the pain that she herself was desperate not to cause. A momentary lapse in emotion was all it took to create a cascade response from the redeemed. Enid became incandescent with guilt, this triggered a reaction from both essences within her, creating a corrosive frothing sensation that was shooting up every nerve. For a moment, her mind was lost in the dissonance between unbearable pain and nothing at all. Through gritted teeth, she growled, looking up at the star.

As she approached the spire, Tij began to feel the charge that constantly emanated from it, the magnetic nature of the spire called to the essences within her. As long as she held the memories she had redeemed she would always be drawn to this place, every part of her was compelled to provide for it, to seek this moment, even if she hated it, hated the way it left her feeling – used, empty, and alone.

Tij's flesh began to prickle and spark, she pushed through the charged and thickening atmosphere that was pulsing in the air like a heartbeat. Reaching out her hand she approached the chair. Upon touching the metal of the spire, the sick sensation fell away from her, the charge that ran through her skin dispersed upon contact with the chair; it had a nullifying effect like a lightning rod. A layer of peace descended on her that only ritual ever provided.

Keeping one hand on the chair, loathe to surrender the stabilising effect it had, Tij felt the peculiar nature of its surface, the raised pattens and the occasional sharp tendrils, which caused her to bleed from deep cuts, drawing rivulets of blood that poured down her fingers. This pain was still better than the sickening atmosphere that would affect her should she let go. Tij positioned herself and sat down.

The force that had drawn her here grabbed hold of every atom within, penetrating with tendrils of cold, razor-sharp energy that coursed along every nerve, seeking out the memories of the essences, distilling what was Tij and what was not. This included alien elements that could restrict her usefulness to the sphere – illness, ageing, anything that did not correspond to a template that the spire held of her previous visit, everything else was removed.

Tij felt the sharp heat surge toward the partition inside her where the redeemed were held. What she carried with her was about to be taken away, brought out into the world, and lost forever.

Time practised, this ritual protected who and what she was, not out of kindness but of efficiency. To ease this process, Tij had long ago learnt to set aside, within her, the essences she had redeemed, but it was impossible to separate herself fully from those she loved, from Enid. The essences the spire would seek out and take held separate within Tij, it was a disconnection that even familiarity and empathy could not bridge. But there were connections that could not be severed, where deep emotional connection simply could not be separated from Tij and as such, when the transfer would happen, the smallest part of Tij would go with the harvest, with Enid, as it did with all the others she had loved. In this way absence and loss were the only things in the sphere that left a mark on Tij. In an existence tied to purpose, to relentlessly ensure continuance, this was a change that was hers alone, and as the paths meandered and carved their way across the concaved face of the world, so grief defined her. It was evidence of a life.

In this place, sitting on the chair at the base of the spire at the edge of the Blissed field, surrounded by empty and hungry Blissed, all dancing to the song of absence, freed from worry and care, Tij watched. A part of her bitterly envied their freedom from grief, of pain, but the cost was unthinkable. Allowing herself to dwell one final time, Tij could think back and recall so much that she had felt and lost, the memories were razor-sharp wires wrapped around her, cutting into her very existence, but these wires also created a circuit that was unique to her; the same wires that bit deeply could carry joy. Tij's tears were both for loss but also a celebration that she had something worthy enough to mourn.

Looking up at the spire, Tij could see in a single gaze, the spire, the engine and the star, all in alignment. Tij felt the spire's magnetic force as it reached into her very being, filling the void between atoms with static, channelled by circuits of nerve and sinew. Tij was guiding the pain, not opposing it, as the spire encroached with a ravenous energy that was coursing toward where both Enid and the Seed lay within her. Tij felt their agitation build, different senses stepped in and away from Tij's conscience, each taking its turn to be exposed.

Tij always found this bizarre and disconcerting, and at that moment she could taste a mix of regret and excitement, and it left an aftertaste in her mouth that made her nauseous. It was hard to reconcile the flavours and Tij scowled, spitting the taste away into the sphere, but the taste of rust and lemons remained. In an instant, the beloved essence and the Seed were snatched from her, completely and suddenly. In this new absence, the sense of herself returned as each of her atoms became released, one after the other, and Tij was left in the chair, intact, the taste slowly fading from her mouth.

Tij realised she had her arms outstretched in front of her, a spasm of entreaty wracked through her body, a reaction to the loss, reaching out toward what had been taken from her, but the sphere offered no comfort. Placing her arms back on the rests either side of the chair she looked up at the spire, tracing the pattern of the whorls and vines sweeping upward from the chair where she sat. The pattern snaked its way upward, forming a hollow point that opened flat and held the dark disc above.

# Chapter 7 – Generation Consumed.

The spire began to vibrate in a deep baritone, a lower chord than what preceded it. Tij felt and heard the sound that indicated the next stage was about to begin. All but two of the essences she had collected were churning away in the spire behind her, a harvest of a generation held contained like a silo filled with grain, they numbered in their thousands, and she had given redemption to every one of them.

Twisting wires at the base around Tij were gossamer thin and reacted to the deep resonance, starting to vibrate, filling the air with a growing hiss.

As the wires rose upward, they became thicker and fewer in number the higher they went. Coiled within the silver spire were hundreds of copper threads, slowly becoming brighter and hotter, generating a charged atmosphere that surrounded Tij in a suffocating embrace.

Tij leant back in the chair, banging her head against the dense metal, and strained her neck to watch the last essences, one of these was her lover, both lighting their separate paths along the vibrating copper wires, on their journey to the very top of the spire. The hot atmosphere and buzzing wires that had surrounded her rose with them, churning the air in a storm of dust.

All the redeemed forged their own pathway up the spire, the journey that all would take was entirely unique. Tij knew one of the bright threads making its way to the top of the spire was Enid, one took a faster route the other seemed reluctant, meandering its way to oblivion. Tij hoped this was Enid, but she did not know.

Tij felt hollow, light-headed and shivered despite the warm air around her. The scant control over her emotions finally failed, there was no one left to be strong for, her grief scuttled out of the deep dark place it had been banished to, and with every heartbeat spread through her body like wildfire through a tinder-dry forest.

The pinnacle of the spire above the dark disc began to glow, signifying that Enid's passing was complete, her journey to the oblivion she so desperately sought concluded.

The spire's glow increased to a burning white light, the buzzing wires swelled in a crescendo, the air crackled with energy. Tij felt the hairs on her arms and neck rise with her heartbeat; the air was stifling and tasted of metal.

This mechanical ritual indicated to the engine that the harvest was ready for collection, its call was always answered, the engine would always come.

Tij slumped forward in the chair, redemption took its toll on the confessor and the Blissed alike. Tears poured down her face, she released her grief from its threadbare reins, and as it ran free it overwhelmed each sense in turn with a dull, ice-cold weight turning raw nerve to heavy lead.

The transfer to the engine would soon be complete. She looked away from the brightening disc at the pinnacle of the spire. The world was alive with sparks, light, heat and sound, but she was numb, no longer feeling anything external to herself, merely enduring it. Part of her had gone with Enid, and all the others she had ever loved before. Tij closed her eyes, releasing a final tear. The inevitability of grief made it no less bearable.

Tij looked across at Meco, he was a shaking silhouette in the storm, their duty complete, purpose fulfilled, but she could see this did not calm him, all the effort, the thankless eternity of competence, of duty, extracts a toll and the salvation of a completed harvest would be fleeting for them both.

They were the same age, but where Meco's scars were plain to see, her wounds were not, they were deep and hidden, and every redemption inflicted a fresh wound, tearing open all the ones that preceded it.

On the sphere, Tij and Meco and the austere and distant occupants of the engine would remember this moment, and the lives surrendered to make it happen. The sphere was cleansed of a generation of Blissed and those sacred relics and souvenirs that their lives created.

Tij knew that all lives are made of small things and small moments, the objects those who are cherished have touched made irreplaceable by the loss of the one who created them. She used to dismiss such thinking as sentimental, but once grief leaves, this is all that is left.

It was this moment Tij's eyes locked onto Meco, who obviously took this as an invitation to approach, shambling toward her and holding himself in an embrace as if trying to hold in all his misery.

Meco stood before her. 'Is it over?' he growled, his mouth agape, 'Can I rest?'

Tij lifted herself from the chair, steadied herself and then stepped toward him. He retreated at first, but Tij quickened her steps, grabbing his hand, feeling his grip tighten as she pulled him close. She traced the scars that formed his face.

Meco placed his gnarled hands upon her shoulders, looking at her elegant face, worn by time and emotion.

As he stared into the soft grey eyes of redemption, all he was capable of seeing was his own loneliness reflected back at him.

'Yes, go and sleep.' She pushed him gently away. Tij's was the burden of continuance, her purpose to create renewal, this would be a beginning that was like all the others, still it was a beginning, nonetheless. A new world would grow from the old to seduce her away from misery back to the intolerable suffering of hope.

The sphere would return to life and each possibility was a salve that eased but did not cure, all that remained was the engine to play its part and the star to restart the world.

Meco did not move and continued to stare; Tij had no more songs for him, no more words. This was the time when the sphere was most at peace, when the Blissed would be renewed, the star fed, and the Seeds left alone in their dreaming shells and Meco does not have to crawl around the depths of the sphere hunting them. Tij knew this to be true, this was a brief liberation for Meco, one of reflection for Tij. She held his stare, they both stood in long silence until Meco turned and walked away.

A shadow passed over them both, as the engine hovered overhead, drawn by the disc still shining at the tip of the spire. The engine made no sound, but its presence drew the surrounding atmosphere toward it causing the swirling wind to rush upward, whistling as it twisted around the scoured surface of the bright, graceful spire.

Tij followed Meco's gaze, he was looking upward to the descending engine. The shadow the engine cast was always the same, the shape of the engine was two circles linked by a thin pylon that resembled an hourglass.

The engine positioned itself above the spire and landed soundlessly through the dying gusts of wind on the flat disc at the apex of the spire. It reminded Tij of a bee landing on a flower in search of pollen. Like a bee, the engine had always followed the same pattern; it was a dance long perfected and slavishly adhered to.

The spire flickered briefly, beginning to dull as sparks poured into the engine from the disc, fingers of searing white lightning dug into the frame of the engine, filling the air with the scent of ozone. The bolts held the engine in a grip that seemed to tighten as the flow of energy grew, building to a caustic brilliance that intensified even the smallest shadow, and then the light was gone.

Enid had gone with the sparks, she was now part of a greater thing, all her memories were just elements, part of the harvest of thousands given redemption and stored in the spire, a harvest the engine collected as fuel for the star.

During the transfer of the harvest the sphere was silent, the air completely still carried only light and shadow.

Tij hated the cold severity of the harvest's final act, its mechanical nature, all memories were fuel, the chaff. The vacant Blissed danced in their shining field, their arms lifted in supplication and adoration to the star. Looking at this scene, Tij saw it as any common crop field after any given harvest: scruffy, bare and forlorn. She felt a surge of disgust at their vacant adoration of absence, shameless, guiltless and greedy for the new lives, shapes and forms that awaited them, a reward for their offering.

The engine slowly ascended, moving from a horizontal position to a vertical then lifted away from the spire heading for the star.

The borrowed darkness of the engine's shadow was disconcerting for Tij, the absence of light was welcome, but it made its eventual return more jarring.

Tij saw Meco looking at the floor and she heard him sigh loudly and mutter something under his breath.

As the engine approached the star it slowed, currents of electricity could be seen running along its glass and metal surface in jagged swirls and vortices, a swarm of elements, an aurora at play, their distinct flows slowing their motion from frenetic to calm in reaction to the approach of the star.

Standing in the shadow of the engine, Tij and Meco were on the leeward side of the bright chaos of the star. Closing one of her eyes, Tij focused on the corona of the star that shone around the partial eclipse caused by the engine. She watched as the burning flares of the corona were drawn toward the engine.

The star's surface, usually so erratic, was now made up of a pattern of lines, each pointing toward the engine and the harvest that was its meal like iron nails pointing toward a magnet.

All movement on the star's surface paused, and as the flows ceased their movement, the light of the star began to dim. The light and heat generated by the star was created by the churning motions of the flow of the ribbons of light as they chased the memories that were almost gone; the light was starving.

The star was not sentient, there was nothing of the star that was not dependant on the sphere to exist, it was a colony of consumed elements, all swirling in constant flow. Still, the star contained within it every thought and dream that the sphere had known. It was true that it would give some of this back to the Blissed that waited in their field as promised, a part of every harvest had to be re-sown, but most it would consume.

Tij gritted her teeth and watched the ravenous star react to the approach of the generation she had redeemed from the world, it was a relentlessly hungry parasite, one that they all depended on for survival.

The dimming of the star was not stark and swift, but it was profound, the whole sphere paused, every branch, leaf and blade of grass was hushed and still, the air and tides sat heavy on the surface of the sphere, the birds and animals hushed. It was a reaction to the threat of this alien darkness, however brief, that brought an awed thrill to every fibre of their collective being, sparking within each of them the need to flee, but to where? There was no escape or respite on this sphere, even the Seeds deep in the ground never escaped the influence of the star.

Shadows on the sphere grew like glaciers, pouring back into the world from unseen sources, and as the light lessened, all the edges of the sphere were softened, less defined, less real.

Tij watched the shadow creep across the Blissed field. All the Blissed there were glowing slightly, all hollow now, bereft of their own memories, their collective embers mere reflections of the star, ghosts of who they used to be.

The Blissed continued to dance in their anticipation of the renewal to come, the shadow meant nothing to them. With the sphere dimmed they appeared all the brighter, illumination is relative.

Each of the Blissed was no less hungry for their share of the promise of the re-sown memories from the star that would renew them than the star was itself. The Blissed began to form lines, reflecting the corona of the star above, every one of them staring upward, all tied to this ritual and the meal of a new life that was about to follow. Once the star had its fuel, they would have theirs, it had always been so.

Tij did not know, could never know, anything of what the Blissed were soon to experience. Renewal needed an ending, and she was constant.

Tij stared across at the Blissed in their lines where once they stood unique, once each walked the sphere with their own personalities, needs and wants. Here they stood in unison, unthinking and ravenous.

This was a terrible creation; a new world would grow from this moment. For Tij, it was at the beginning of the world when it was most alive, when everything was uncertain and new. Once the Blissed received their gift of a new life, all would begin again, all new life springs from the bones of the old one. New forms, new people would be reborn into the sphere, at first all of them would be awkward and uncertain, free for a time to explore their new lives, they would grow the gift given them by the star into lives that had never been lived.

Tij would let her grief take hold, seeking isolation at first to spend time with the ruined keep sakes and Enid-worn objects she had gathered and collected, but it would be impossible to keep herself distant; Tij would be drawn toward the fresh lives walking the old world.

Loneliness would draw her from her grieving solace. Tij would feel the pull to be involved in noise and chaos, where she was part of something that was beyond her purpose, where she could be seen as a person, even for a short time.

In Tij's long life she had found that the only thing that was a salve to grief was life. As everything else it would follow a predictable pattern, life would be all innocent at first, each moment was one of discovery and wonder and Tij felt that renewal vicariously.

The Blissed would keep near to Tij, they needed to have redemption at hand, the merest hint of any pain brought by this new experience of life caused the weakest of them to seek the escape only she could provide.

She had been lover and friend over the cycles, but she had redeemed them all without exception. The nascent beginning would be raw, but it was never long before life flourished. Beginnings and endings were always the hardest, life always followed the same pattern.

Tij knew that what would follow this beginning was the closest Meco could get to peace. As the new forms of the Blissed would eventually solidify, as personalities settled and confidence grew, curiosity drove the timid Blissed to wander, this would soon become the high tide that drew around his seclusion.

The Blissed explored the world with trepidation, as if stricken by curiosity, not freed by it. They tentatively crept among the ruins of the towns, the fields and rivers, lakes, and rail, rarely leaving the confines of where the previous harvests had lived. New crop, same field.

Tij had seen Meco track the new Seeds, it was the best way for him to maintain distance; he did not want them close; their naivety angered him. It also gave him a chance to categorise them. He always knew the ones who would run, who would be among the first to seek redemption, and he was rarely wrong. Meco's only solace was that he would have some time in isolation before the next harvest would need supplementing through the hunt, at least before the wanderings of the new, refilled Blissed interrupted his peace, either through proximity or as prey.

The shadow the engine cast was diffuse, made fuzzy by the charged atmosphere that had followed the harvest from the spire to the engine. Everywhere else on the sphere was brighter outside the shadow, even under the light of the dimming star the shadow felt like an aura around them, framing where Meco and Tij both stood in a hazy air that created an increasingly diffused border between light and dark that was unique to itself, something that was not completely one or the other.

Directly above them the star continued to react to the approach of the engine, all the lines of flow, every mark seen on the star's bright-yellow surface, was pointing toward the engine. It was as if the star itself was intently looking at its approaching meal. The dimming light was amplified by the reflective surface of the Blissed field, which was now the brightest point anywhere on the spheres surface.

The sphere, spire, engine and star all aligned; the stage was set.

Pointing toward the engine, the flows were straining to reach beyond the surface of the star causing its corona to expand, its cohesion becoming lost as it reached out. The corona split into threads, each one a flare that had its root in the star but stretched outward toward the approaching engine, bright yellow at its base and orange at its apex.

It was not long before the flares were level with the engine, halfway between the star and the Blissed field.

All the flares were united in motion but independent in form, creating a tunnel of diagonal lines that reached past its meal in the engine, it resembled a grotesque, elongated maw of a colossal beast.

As the flare neared the Blissed field its influence on those waiting there was profound. The Blissed were beyond glow and heat, they were now molten.

Like the border of the diffuse shadow cast by the star they were neither one thing nor the other, all the unique features that set them apart were gone, each a pure iridescent shape, contorted into a new state of reflective silver. All that mattered to them was what was emanating from the star, which soon would set the terms and forms of their new lives.

Dark orange motes floated through the air, growing in number as the star crept toward the engine. The Blissed field shone brightly and every living thing on the sphere was still except the Blissed, the engine, and the star above, which was reaching down toward them as the engine edged ever closer. The weight of the star pressed down on both Tij and Meco. The pressure of the air changed causing both of Tij's ears to pop. What she wanted from this moment was different from Meco, but they both wanted this to end, they were both caught between an irretrievable past and an inevitable future.

Tij had carried every memory that was within the engine. Inside were thousands of lives she herself had delivered to the spire, which the engine had drained, to be served up, consumed, shattered, broken then fused, in an explosive reaction that created all the light and heat that washed over the living sphere.

The fusion also created new elements, these would combine in the churning furnace of the star, reforged into the new memories and lives that would be re-sown to the hungry Blissed.

This generation will soon be consumed. Tij watched as their vacant forms danced in the light of the sacrifice of those that went before them, just as the next generation will dance in theirs.

Tij felt a deep sadness for a world full of people now lost, but it was shallow compared to the void inside her that was her grief for Enid, the beautiful iridescent person that she was, her quirks and habits, the life they'd had together and the life they could have had. This was the life Enid had begged Tij to take from her, to release her from agony that had consumed her like a wildfire.

There were echoes of guilt as well, for not putting an end to Enid's anguish sooner, but she just could not bear to let her go, to be alone in the world, again, but here she was, watching her lover, a blended part of a generation ascending in the engine toward the star, in an inevitable cycle that turned like a heavy wheel, crushing all she cared about, the wheel of progress oiled by her misery and loss.

Every tomorrow is a revolution, a victory over the past, and all revolutions demand the sacrifice of a generation to fuel it.

Those who survive the chaos will live to see the next generation dance in the light it created by that sacrifice, oblivious to its cost, not its promise ... Tij understood both.

# Chapter 8 – Orbits are Merely Habit.

Fingers of searingly bright white energy held the engine in a radiant grasp, each spark and crackle signifying the transfer of the harvest to the engine, every second was a life.

The silver surface of the spire and Blissed reflected the light of the approaching yellow star. The maw of twisted orange flares, the intermittent flashes of white flowed in breathing colours, each individual curve of form creating an abstraction of the story of change unfolding above them.

In the engine, all systems were primed and ready for the arrival of the harvest. Robot plugged each tendril into the filtration mechanism between the two vats of pollution, spreading itself like a web, connecting every part of the engine.

The harvest coursed into the engine from the spire below in a series of white-hot spikes of energy that spread along every metal surface of the engine; this was the harvest in its raw unfiltered state.

The engine glowed with the force of the harvest. All the memories of a generation were present, sadness and joy mixed together with every emotion in between, only the lighter elements would be used as fuel, the process of separating light fuel and the heavy elements of pollution was a simple one. Robot served as the engine's filter.

A loop of wire was formed along a track, a small amount of pure fuel held within as bait.

Robot knew from programme and experience that each element sought itself, joy sought joy, misery likewise sought misery, but joy was so much swifter.

Robot entered the final command into the system that caused the loop of wires to move in a circle around the circumference of the engine. Its bait of bright joy triggered an immediate reaction, all the elements of the harvest hunted the bait at first, but only the lighter elements could keep up with its prey.

As Robot quickened the loop, the lighter elements within the harvest kept pace, becoming stretched into a swarm of bright ribbons like golden threads being pulled from a dark tapestry. Quickening the loop ever faster continued to purify the fuel, filling the engine with gossamer-thin ribbons that coiled around each other like a murmuration of starlings, brightening each time they touched, growing brighter and hotter.

The engine was filled with pure unendurable joy. Robot knew from its intolerance and programming that the specified level had been reached, changing the speed of the wire circle once more to weave the filtered harvest into a long chain, each link forged from a ribbon of light.

It was a structure that required the least amount of contact between the still brightening ribbons, reducing the danger of explosion.

The bright chain was formed into loops, resembling the burning nervous system of some great beast. With a spark of command, Robot sent the fuel forward toward the front of the engine, watching it pour through the aperture between its two parts, along the pylon, which brightened like the element in a light bulb for Control to prepare the fuels transfer to the star.

All that was left behind was the heavy residue of sadness, the part of the harvest that had been filtered gravitated to itself, becoming slower and denser, transformed into a black, unguent liquid that resembled tar.

The process of filtration ceased, Robot stopped the movement of the loop and the bait of joy it contained, and the pollution that was left over was no longer capable of chasing such a rarefied thing.

Pollution slowly gathered at the floor of the engine, dripping down the glass and metal walls until all of it lay like a shallow viscous pool in which Robot saw its own reflection on the oily surface.

Joy had value in that it fed the star, but this pollution fed Robot, sadness lets you dream.

To move the pollution to the vats, Robot whispered a story of change along the wires of the frame, offering the sadness that it craved more than joy ... meaning.

Slow but relentless, the pollution crawled up the wires, absorbing the story that was transmitted as it went until it met the tendrils of Robot, who guided it toward the vats that were full to the brim.

A scream of static resonated from Control along the hard surfaces of glass and metal. The tone and ferocity hit Robot like a bolt of lightning, who now bathed in the pollution of sadness; it not only felt but understood.

Control's pain was a consequence of sacrifice born from logic and maladapted empathy, all drawn from the pollution shared by Robot, drawn from generations of harvests. It hurt, not in the way that nerves and flesh do but the breakdown of a system, a rending divergence of purpose and programming. An apt comparison was if someone tore flesh from themselves fighting against their own survival instinct to keep existing. Control was not rendering itself surgically, it could not, its programming would not allow it.

Robot unplugged itself from the filter as the last of the pollution poured into the vats, which began to overflow and burst through their containment. Removing the book from its core, Robot pressed it into the aperture between it and Control, recording the story of the suffering of the system that governed the sphere. Robot had shared its awakening with Control, now together they would share its consequence.

The screaming static abated. Robot gathered the book with pollution slick tendrils and placed it back inside its frame, looked through the glass of the engine and saw the star open, awaiting their approach. All the ribbons of light that made up the star were still, making the surface of the star appear to be made up of burning scars.

Each wound was a ribbon of light reaching upward, forming a tunnel that surrounded the engine. This journey had been taken countless times, but Robot felt the shiver of disquiet spark along its tendrils.

The tunnel of ribbons of light stretched out from the star and as they did so it caused the star in front of the engine to split open and separate, like the gaping maw of a colossal beast. The light there was becoming dull, rising, and falling slightly, like a slowing heartbeat.

Robot could see into the very centre of the star. Every layer of light brightened as it neared the core, and in its current form the core is a withered thing. This would be the repository of the harvest, the feeding trough for the star, and it had been picked clean, fully consumed, and it demanded renewal.

Control steered the engine closer, releasing a single spark of the filtered fuel. It was a signal to the star, prompting a response from the swarm of ribbons that the star consisted of. Robot thought this stage of the process resembled a ringing bell to a herd of cattle, indicating it was feeding time.

The signal triggered a surge of motion as each of the ribbons responded, causing the star to move further from its central position, closer toward the engine and the Blissed field below. The change in movement caused a cascade of flares to be ejected from the tunnel that reached out from the star, a reaction from the surge of movement from the ribbons.

Robot watched the flares snake their way down the tunnel of ribbons, which now completely surrounded the engine. As the cascade of flares reached the end of the tunnel below the engine, the flares hit the Blissed field below in a sequence of looping threads of fire and light, thrown from the tunnel that stretched from the surface of the star.

They hit the Blissed field in waves, each bringing the promise of new memories re-sown to the willing Blissed, who supplicated themselves entirely to this cycle of re-creation. Even from this height, Robot saw how they melted and merged, reformed, and separated.

Their very beings voraciously absorbing the star's gift, taking this into the very centre of themselves.

The Blissed were all molten, infused with the gift of a new life. Their forms were processing into new shapes, new flesh, each of the Blissed were becoming a new being. Anything of their former existence was gone forever. They were as bright as they were nondescript. This is the fate they sought as willing components of a ritual that they dedicated their very existence to ensure. All was as it had ever been.

The engine approached the star and there was a mutual effect. The filtered fuel that sat at the front of the engine coursed around Control in caustically bright threads that burnt ever brighter as the star neared.

The pollution that Robot had drip-fed into the system was part of Control and was repelled by the bright emotion held in the fuel, water to the oil of pollution.

Robot reached for the book once more, placing it back on the pollution that filled the aperture between Robot and Control, this pain must be shared, nothing will be missed, this story would serve as the epitaph for a system, one that had kept everything that drew breath and charge on the sphere alive, at such terrible cost it was true, but the fact the sphere was alive to contemplate such tyranny was the legacy of Control.

Robot drew the book away, the transmission from Control had lost coherence, reduced to the static of desperate cries rendered from the need for self-annihilation. Control was being torn apart by what it had become, a blend of ritual programme and alien emotion and what it must do to give the sphere a chance of survival. In the end, even emotion is a matter of a series of equations leading to an inevitable conclusion.

Through the resonance of static, Robot felt the crack in the pylon between the two parts of the engine, then the sudden change in gravity as the rear part fell toward the sphere.

Suspended in the air of the sphere, Robot saw Control in the front of the engine continue its ascent to the star, bristling with the harvest as the maw of the star began to close around it.

In the disconnection from Control, the screaming was silenced and for the first time, Robot felt alone, detached, an isolated entity, in sudden descent, saturated in the pollution of sadness filtered from a generation.

The rear part of the engine fell down toward the sphere. Robot was awash with heavy sensations of borrowed suffering mixed with the ecstasy of falling as it flowed through every element, every cable and atom, it was a potent sensation, a vortex all being absorbed more than understood. All churning around inside its metal form, and for those moments of descent, at the point where the balance between self and pollution became uncertain, Robot was lost in the manic forms of chaos.

It was all flow but no direction. Sensations were colliding and slowing, but each of these new flecks of experience lacked any kind of pattern, they coiled around in sudden currents that were as bright as they were fleeting, each collision generated a flash of story or song, an emotion never before felt or experienced, all forged from chaos and friction.

When Robot's part of the engine approached the sphere, it slowed and gently touched the ground at the edge of the Blissed field. The silence in the engine was absolute.

Testing the return of gravity with tentative steps, Robot moved toward the ill-used door pressing a tendril into the mechanism and watched as the door spun open, hesitating, suddenly aware of its vulnerability before taking the final few steps of its descent.

Standing, Robot began a swift inventory of the objects and pollution stored behind it in the engine. All was as it should be, this was a precious cargo, there was no guarantee that such unique creations could ever repeat or replenish, common things reach a level of deification either by time or rarity, the former a consequence of the latter. All these kept and treasured things could bring such a harvest like none yet seen or felt and all that Robot had curated had survived and sat ready in its given place.

Tij watched the predictable dance of the engine and star play out above, its effect on the sphere, though profound, was merely part of the ritual around the harvest. The darkening light cast strange, blurred shadows, the rushing wind whipped her hair around her neck, even the rare spectacle of the star's approach held little interest.

The dimming yellow star was mirrored by the surface of the field, reflected in the dancing forms of the molten Blissed who swayed and shifted, awash in the new lives their bodies were converting from the gift of the star. It was a renewal, but it looked like motes trapped in the dying embers of a fire.

Tij could no longer see Enid. The thought of her lover brought a rush of grief that took her breath away. Tij was glad she could not see; it was impossibly difficult to watch the one you love dissolve into an unrecognised form.

Light above and below her, Tij stepped away from the edge of the Blissed field. It always made her dizzy, a horizon made of light, its blurred edges were suffocating.

Meco cried, it was a deep and guttural roar, just another part of the ritual, the emotion it conveyed was fear and relief. Tij looked across at Meco who was stood closer to her than she remembered, he was looking up, Tij followed his gaze.

The engine had split in two and the rear part was descending toward them soundlessly through the swirling air, the glass of its surface refracting the light into curved shards of violet and red. Meco had made his way to Tij's side, but Tij did not take her eyes from the engine. She saw Meco move, through the corner of her eye, to stand in front of her, setting himself between Tij and the engine as it landed on the edge of the Blissed field.

Seconds were refracted into eternity as Tij stepped forward to stand beside Meco and they both peered into the glass and metal frame. There was too much light and tears, nothing could be seen clearly. The wall in front of them dimmed slightly, moved back into the engine, and then rolled away to reveal a mass of oily coils and tendrils that tightened into a vaguely human shape, which stood in front of them for a silent minute and then rushed forward to stand halfway between Meco, Tij and the engine.

The surface of Robot was shifting and seemed to be shivering. A twist of tendrils that resembled a hand reached out from the coiled form and sharply pointed to the star above them.

The star reacted as it always had; the bright ribbons began to slowly turn around the core, vying for a place within for the feast that was to come.

Control's part of the engine increased in brightness; it was the signal to the star for the feast to commence. The light was piercing. Control itself was soon brighter than the star had ever been, a pure brilliance that caused the star to fall on the sphere as a shadow, which fell around Tij like a heavy cloak.

This brilliance was irresistible to the ribbons within the star, their speed increased as the maw slowly closed around the beleaguered shining part of the engine that was Control.

Tij was torn between her confusion and rising fear of a robot looming over both her and Meco, and relief that the harvest was over. She smiled nervously, tears flowing down her face, her mind spun in a state of frenzy, reactions to the end of a life driven by intense grief and unashamed relief. She breathed deeply. The robot and new sky above her were precious moments of uncertainty. Eagerly, she awaited the new life that was about to unfold.

Standing beside her, Meco was not smiling, his frame taught and awkward, his face scowled, and he continued to mutter to himself as he stared darkly at the robot, who was unmoving, completely intent on the star above.

The churn of ribbons on the star's surface moved faster, the friction of their movement generated light and heat in response to the signal from Control. The bright harvest was causing this worn ritual to become something else. The speed increased as the brightness of the star matched the incandescence of Control. The star began to increase in size, the powerful invections feeding the expansion, the light and heat building as the flows of the ribbons of light quickened. The star swelled like a blister.

The Blissed responded. Tij saw their molten and starving forms reach higher, arms almost tentacle-like in their effort, stretched toward the star as it grew in size and proximity toward them and the sphere. Their molten bodies glowed, then burnt, their radiance matched the star, each in a state of absolute mania.

Meco placed a hand on Tij's shoulder, pulling her gently away from the robot, but she swatted his hand away. The sphere held its collective breath in silent reverence as the star approached, and then exhaled. Birds and insects swarmed around the sky seeking shelter. All animals of the sphere, truer to their nature than the Blissed, were driven to escape, stampeding through forests and whipping the air into strobing shadows against the light, creating forms driven by the wind that was hurtling around the sphere. Meco removed his hand but did not take his eyes from the robot, and he stayed by Tij's side.

Trees shivered, walls crumbled, the lakes and rivers frothed with terrified life, tortured by the savage light to seek depths that had never been there to reach.

The storm escalated as the star expanded, all was screaming in utter tumult, the Blissed in anticipation, and held enrapt in terror. The Blissed were processing the new forms that the end of the harvest had brought them, the end, the storm, the light, all this was a final flurry of the promised gift of renewal.

Clarity comes at the point of absolute uncertainty, when weaker material held within is boiled away leaving the strongest elements, the most precious things, exposed and gleaming.

Tij ignored the tumult around her and remained focused on the star. The chaos in the world was a consequence of change and impossible for her to care about. She held her hand close over the void just below her heart, lost in reverie. Tij heard Meco charge at the robot and the dull sickening thud of flesh hitting metal. She watched as he got back to his feet clumsily, shaking her head slightly as he stared at the ground and grumbled to himself, shifting his position slightly to move from the shadow of the robot.

# Chapter 9 – Sisyphus Stops.

The sphere, battered by the storm caused by the proximity of the engorged star was still lit by its failing light as it approached its perigee. The internal motion that created light and heat was stilled and consequently the light of the star was reduced to a dull orange; the deep layers of ribbons darkened in colour the deeper they went. Each ribbon was ravenous, awaiting the fuel from the harvest to consume, the last offering at its heart was all but spent. The frenzied motion of the ribbons that made the star were now stilled, each snake like ribbon was waiting to strike.

The placement of the harvest was key, it was all that kept the star in a cohesive form. The ribbons would always seek the fuel, the star was not a solid form but a swarm of hungry ribbons of light as they fed, tearing apart the lives and experiences sacrificed to them. New memories were formed for the future, all light and heat that the sphere needed to survive was generated by the relentless flow of the ribbons as they fought, collided, and rushed past each other to get to the harvest that would soon be delivered to its heart.

The star opened itself to receive the shining harvest from Control. Tij could see all the way to its withered heart and the scraps that were all that was left of the last harvest. This was the beast that Tij's grief had fed, it was this beast that she served to ensure the continuance of the sphere. She watched as every ribbon was pointing toward the harvest, these ragged flows were straining to reach beyond the surface of the star, its cohesion becoming lost the more it reached out. Tij could see through in places to the other side of the sphere.

Tij understood this display for what it was – a threat. The great swarm was readying itself, like a snake rearing its head before striking its prey, the tunnel of flares an extended, wide-open mouth that surrounded Control and the harvest.

The force of wind was driven by the star's approach, the air being propelled through the narrowing gap between the sphere's surface and the star. Tij turned her head away for a moment and saw the effect the sphere was having on the crops and forests; it was like a hand being rubbed across velvet.

Control ascended to the star, its corrupted purpose the burning apex of its programming, filled with the harvest, the fuel of continuance, which will light the future. It hovered in the air above Tij, Meco and the robot; a dark smudge against the dimming maw of the star that surrounded its meal.

The engine was broken, Control was alone in the air for the first time, this was terrifying enough, the careful, deliberate descent of the robot made the whole scene worse. There was purpose here, it was planned.

Despite the unprecedented presence of the robot, it was impossible for Tij to be anywhere else, this was where she had always stood, this is where redemption had always witnessed the birth of a new generation, nothing would change that.

Meco's reaction was predictable, she could hear him moan and curse, and felt his hand on her shoulder trying to gently pull her away. Tij angrily broke free and glowered at the robot. The ritual was as much a way for her to exorcise her grief as much as it was to restart the world. She refused to let the robot disrupt her process, her recovery was dependent on habit, where she stood, what she felt, she had to remain true and play her part, there was nowhere to run anyway, even if she wanted to.

The oily stench of the robot filled the air that swirled around them. Tij could see a broken cluster of lenses roughly around where a shoulder would be that seemed fixed upon her, not on Control above.

The star was at its perigee, a bloated parasite that fed the world, now an ember, the ribbons of it surface all still and reaching, out to control. Its approach drove the winds of the sphere into frenzy, it was impossible to hear anything else.

The storm whistled through the fibrous form of the Robot; the air was heavy with its stench that not even the driving wind could disperse.

Dust and soil of the sphere was thrown into Tij. She took a step backwards to rebalance herself. Crouching down, she leant into the storm and returned to the exact spot where she had stood before. Neither the robot nor the sphere itself would rob her of her place in the world.

Dark orange ribbons continued to split through the surface of the star above, resembling a writhing mass of eels, each one brightening and heating up as they pushed past each other vying for the best position to feed from the approaching meal. The maw closed completely around the shining harvest, and this served as the trigger. Flows of ribbons burst through the surface of the star, reaching free of the surface, desperate to find a new way to get to the harvest. Their speed and energy made them clumsy, smashing into each other, causing them to ricochet, each impact making them brighter, swifter, hungrier.

The Blissed field shone in reflective radiance of the reignited star, all the Blissed upon it molten, their old forms and shapes surrendered as they bathed in the gift of light from the star's corona. The surface of the Blissed field was designed with purpose, reflecting the light at the perfect frequency, acting as a lure to draw the star's surface closer. That proximity drew the ribbons of light above them, looping in a series of flares, each made from countless ribbons of light.

Tij endured each wave of heat in turn as another flare struck the Blissed field. When the force struck the Blissed, Tij's heart sank, this was the last goodbye, the memories of Enid were above about to be fed to the star, but the body, the shape of her was gone forever, she could not even tell which one of the molten shapes was her.

Tij closed her eyes as the second flare struck the field. When she opened them she saw that the robot had moved to place itself between her and the stifling heat of the Blissed field.

This was new but was only the precursor to the creeping sense of dread that coursed along Tij's nerves.

'Why is this taking so long?' she shouted at Meco, but her words were as lost in the wind as Meco was lost in his own shadow, and the robot did not answer. 'Why is this taking so long?' she whispered to herself.

The harvest was ascending in the broken engine, so much slower than it would if it had been intact. The delay agitated the hungry star, drawing an increasing number of flares and ribbons, all of which coiled above the bright orange surface, which was becoming threadbare as the ribbons sought a path to the harvest. Tij could see the shrivelled, exhausted heart of the star itself.

Control was gone from view and was hidden by the mass of ribbons that continued to snake around its wounded frame, but Tij could see the effect it was having, first one ribbon struck, then others, this was too soon, the harvest should be at the star's centre. The ribbons struck and they sparked into light as they fought past each other, striking Control in cascades of ravenous intent.

Control plummeted out of the star directly above where Tij stood, and a wave of brightening ribbons followed. Tij fell backwards, her scream lost in the tumult. Lying on her back, she stared, wild-eyed, as the engine, chased by the disintegrating star, hurtled toward her. Control stopped suddenly; its descent so close above her that she could see the glass had been cracked by the assault of the ribbons. Her eyes raw and watery could not look away. Hovering, Control, incandescent and wounded, still full of the harvest, was struck again by the ribbons of light biting into its frame. The screech of tortured metal and glass was akin to the scream of a wounded animal.

White-hot debris fell like rain around Tij as Control shot away to her right, scattering many of the ribbons of light that had latched on to it. The ribbons coiled around each other, becoming brighter and hotter as they pursued Control who flew erratically close to the surface of the sphere.

The star was unravelling, stretched into an elongated, fiery tangle of threads twisting free in the air, each intent on its pursuit of the part of the engine steered with precision by Control. The sundered star was a beast with many heads, each a ribbon of searing white light burning through the air. Tij's tortured eyes reflected the sight. The sphere was filled with whirls of light as the ribbons contorted themselves, each intent on its own hunger, no longer part of a greater thing, ruthless greed had rendered them into selfish separate beings.

Control flew with all the purpose and remorseless drive with which it had governed the sphere. Its path brought it back to the air above the Blissed field pursued by all the denizens of the unwoven star.

The Blissed were struck by the outmanoeuvred ribbons and coils that chased Control. Tij could not tell if their molten forms were contorted from agony or ecstasy. Both the Blissed and the Blissed field shone brighter from the impacts.

The ribbons' frantic hunt of the harvest caused them to fly recklessly, striking at Control and missing, or being flung away by collision with other ribbons that had locked briefly onto the metal surface of the engine before Control scraped them off using the surface of the sphere as grit.

The molten bodies of the Blissed were reacting to the gift of light, memories and experiences that swept through them from the collisions of flare and ribbon, and as the searing threads swept past and through them to rejoin the hunt of Control, the Blissed drank the chaos like nectar.

Standing slowly, Tij could not take her eyes from the spectacle, the passing of the ribbons brought her the closest she had ever been to the star.

The star in its old form was tyrannical in its demands from the sphere, from her, but held within its light and embers were the memories of all those she had loved, and now these memories were everywhere. The searing ribbons were caustic lines burnt into her vision, the driving wind was hot and unbearable.

She could hear and see the flashes of what the threads still held. They passed closely, as they chased Control across the sphere.

The pursuit was not graceful, not a straight line, every thread arced and swirled, flying at Control with the speed of a striking snake. Very few hit their mark, and when a thread missed through the manoeuvrings of Control, the threads hammered into the surface of the sphere, gouging and scarring soil, brick and stone, igniting all it touched: forests, buildings, crops and factories, soon the whole sphere was burning. Light was everywhere.

Ribbons of light swept round and past Tij and for an instant she could hear and feel what they contained. The light and heat were a fusion of the memories and experiences of generations; the star had been kept alive by manically consuming itself, all new material fed to it was how it was tethered to the world and kept useful. Seeing the star that held the world in its tyranny, shredded and wrecking all it once lit, brought a state of freedom that Tij did not understand. She was free from the tyranny of light, but it was a freedom that absolutely held no promise of a tomorrow. It brought a conflicted and mixed state to Tij's mind, more akin to a thrilled grief as it was to terror.

Tij could not predict the path of Control at first, but there was so little free air in which it could fly that was not full of ribbons, each a flow that was surging and thickening through their collisions as they desperately gave chase.

Control was flying much closer to the surface of the sphere where there were still gaps in the air between the light, but the pursuing threads were devastating the sphere, gouging craters and carving scars, all glowing red still from the impact.

The destruction was bad enough, but it was the utter randomness of it. Control was seeking escape. There was no pattern, no rhythm, the sequence, the certainties that once ruled the sphere, neutered, gone.

Through fear, Tij found she was rooting for Control. She watched as Control was almost caught again. Having broken free of its previous capture, the multitude of ribbons were slowly coalescing into a single one. They were being woven by the path of Control into a single massive ribbon, impossibly bright and energetic, here was all that remained of the star.

Tracing the path Control had taken, Tij saw there were sections of the sphere that had been gouged deeply. She could see specks of white against the green of the sphere where the ribbon had struck the surface, becoming caught like rags in branches of a tree, fires spread in a creeping tide of red and orange.

The rush of ash filling the air was pierced by a long sharp scream. The noise was the rending of the engine's metal by the ribbons. All stray light had been drawn into the single broad ribbon. This last flow had caught Control, but Control was still moving at speed, spiralling, and contorting, inverting its path, turning in on itself trying to shake the ribbon loose, and then it headed straight toward the ground opposite Tij, who still stood at the edge of the Blissed field. Tij watched as Control and the ribbon crashed into the abandoned town where Meco had hunted so many Seeds.

She could see the Seeds cast in the air by the impact, scattered and crystalised by the force of Control, and the ribbon of light piling into the surface of the sphere. They glittered in the debris, glowing a deep angry red.

Tij, with terrified slowness, snuck behind the robot, seeking shelter, its unmoving form the only solid thing on the whole sphere close enough for protection.

Tij heard the robot being peppered with rock from the impact. Meco grabbed her leg making her jump; she had forgotten about him. He was screaming toward the devastation, but the air was too heavy and full to carry sound.

Meco grabbed Tij, she pulled away from him, but he was too strong, she kicked out at him as he dragged her from the shelter of the robot. Control had disappeared into the surface of the sphere taking the ribbon that had latched itself hungrily along with it. Tij could see the ribbon, the stretched-out remnant of the star, as it loomed directly above them, coiled around in the air of the sphere.

Meco knelt and placed his hands on the ground trying to feel if Control was going to burst through the surface, but seconds turned to minutes and there was nothing.

Tij could see that the ribbon was going deeper, still intent on its pursuit of Control, which, despite the impact, had not shaken it loose. The light was unceasing in its pursuit of its meal, the ribbon that was once a star hunted Control and the harvest into the very surface of the sphere.

The robot suddenly grabbed Tij, its tendrils wrapped and coiled around her arm, and then in closing orbits around her waist and shoulders, they felt starkly cold and slick, it stunk of oil and corruption. She lashed out, but tendrils coiled around her, restricting any movement other than breathing. The Robot scuttled toward its part of the engine, which was still at the edge of the Blissed field.

The robot's tendrils bit deep into the flesh of her arms and shoulders as she struggled. Meco grabbed her legs, which had become exposed as the robot shifted its coils to move Tij ever closer to the grounded part of the engine. Tij screamed and kicked out at the robot's relentless strength as the tendrils bit deeper. She felt blood trickle down exposed flesh.

Meco released her leg and began pounding on the slick frame of the robot, pushing fingers into its fibrous form, trying to pull it apart, but it was solid, its wires completely unaffected by his attempt. She saw Meco look around for a weapon. Picking up a rock, he struck repeatedly but there was no reaction, not even a sound as the unguent coils that made up the form of the robot remained intact. Tij saw the desperation in Meco's face, he could do nothing but follow the robot, as it continued moving toward the landed part of the engine, trying to spot a way to get Tij free of its embrace.

They approached the fallen engine. The robot swatted Meco aside with a crushing blow and threw Tij inside. She fell hard onto a large pile of broken objects, scattering them as she stood and rushed toward the door.

The robot hesitated briefly and then placed its tendrils along the door, triggering the mechanism to close it. Meco rushed at the robot from behind in a final act of desperation. It turned, thrusting tendrils forward from random points in its form. Every single one struck Meco simultaneously; it was as unyielding as a solid block of metal.

Tij threw herself desperately at the glass door. There was no vibration, no sound when she struck. Winded, she slid to the floor and stared back at the world she was locked away from. The robot was holding Meco in the air, impaled on countless tendrils, he resembled a stricken puppet in silhouette against the burning world. Tij searched around for something to strike the glass, hurriedly moving toward the centre of the engine, toward a pile of objects. Without warning, she was pinned to the floor by the rapid ascent of the engine.

# Chapter 10 – Entanglement.

Pressed to the glass floor by the speed of the ascent, Tij gritted her teeth and felt tears rush from her eyes. Seeking escape back toward the sphere, searing white light poured into the engine as it continued to ascend in opposition to the ribbon still piling its way into the surface of the sphere below.

Tij started to see gaps in the light, as the engine climbed, the ribbon became less cohesive the further away it was from the head that had latched onto Control far below them.

The ribbon was woven from separate flows of light, each with single purpose, to capture and consume the harvest. At the head of the ribbon it clung to Control, a starving predator would never willingly release its prey, focused on its target, the ribbon had cohesion and strength.

Tij travelled upward beside the ribbon. She could see through the glass walls of the engine the single ribbon becoming threadbare, so far from its prey. The ribbon split into a web of chaotic threads, stretching across the air, and then the light ended.

An end? Tij was witnessing the last part of the star spread out like gossamer across the air. There were fewer gaps large enough for the engine to fly through to avoid the burning ribbons.

The engine shook violently as it was caught in the fiery web, Tij was trapped in the shredded remains of the star. The engine was instantly filled with dazzling colours as the glass of the engine served as a prism. The ribbons were created by flows, flows were woven from memories, all relics of countless harvests all shredded by the churn within the star, then fused into bright new elements created from the memories of past generations, smashing into, or consuming one another, as part of a flow of a greater thing.

Motes hovered in front of Tij, twisting in the air as they would above a fire, bright and stark, still connected to the gossamer threads through the transmission of light.

Tij could only watch, helpless as the motes began eating each other, swarming like locusts, there was no other fuel, and they were ravenous.

The motes' purpose here was the same as the ones at the head of the ribbon – collide and consume – but here at the frayed end, a position they found themselves in purely by chance, that purpose was becoming corrupted by unsatiated hunger for the harvest it chased but was so far away from.

The air filled with the swarm of motes as they scoured the engine, delving into the objects, but there was not enough to gorge themselves upon. Tij felt a rush of fear, as the motes swerved around the black liquid seeping from the vats. She knew their intent. Tij felt each mote bite into her, invading her own memories, their greed switched from the pursuit of the harvest to the bounty of memories within Tij.

As the motes delved deeper, they collided with her subconscious. They were digging around Tij's mind, the light had always sought to invade, but now it sought to consume.

Still pinned to the floor of the engine by velocity, Tij could feel herself burrowed into and torn from the inside. The pain was excruciating, but it was everywhere, there was no specific part of her that felt ease. Tij could not focus, there was a myriad of alien experiences hitting her, visceral shrapnel of lives long gone, voices, feelings, all dislocated and without context, the motes were a torrid storm of super liminal consciousness, powerful, searing joy, and they were ravenous.

The bright memories were alien, the toxin of a parasite intent on its assault. All sense of her felt exposed and raw, her life was a collective of events and purpose, a constituency of memory and experience, and it was this that the motes were seeking as they burrowed deeper, leaving her completely alone, in confusion and agony, lost in a light that was never a friend but was now intent on consuming her.

Flailing around, Tij's arms pushed through the many objects that were scattered on the floor of the engine, incapable of thought, just feeling. The sensation of objects as she pushed through and past them barely registering in her mind, her flesh cut by the shattered glass and splinters of the objects as she was wounded once again by the remnants of a once greater thing.

Light crept everywhere; the motes dived into every part of her in their search for scraps of bright memory to sustain them. Tij felt what they sought; they wanted the sugar rush from bright memory, the energy gained from consuming heavier, deeper elements was released slower, but the light needed something instant, sweet, and bright. Tij was the only morsel they could find. They began to ravage and consume, her mind swept along with the joy-bright motes as they continued to chase the memories around inside her, centring them to make them easier to catch, like a dolphin hunting fish. Focusing, Tij tried the rituals she knew to push the light away, to redraw the borders, but what use were borders in a flood?

In the space of three deep breaths, the engine and all it held was weightless, as it hit the zenith of its ascent. The strands and motes still ensnared the engine in the wake of the ribbon that was once the star. In that instant, everything the engine contained was floating free and Tij fought to regain herself, the weightlessness only adding to her beleaguered sense of isolation and fear.

The engine reached the end of the ribbon and the last tendrils coiled around the engine, dragging both Tij and the engine down along with it into the surface.

Tij, with all the other objects, was hurled to the opposite side by the engine's new direction. A deep crack resonated through the air as the engine was dragged by Control and the ribbon that was smashing a path through the sphere. The sound hit Tij like a blow. Opening her eyes, she saw the black unguent pollution pour toward her.

Tij was swamped in the dark pollution left in the engine, like a flood it was filled with debris, glass and splinters, which sparkled through the black liquid.

The invasive motes still dug into Tij, she could feel the joyful memories radiating from them, all so bright and sharp, she was being eviscerated.

Her screams were stolen by the pollution that poured down her throat, it was a bitter metallic taste that made Tij wretch and convulse. She began to panic, fear of being torn apart replaced by the terror of drowning.

The motes chewing their way through her reacted to the effect of the pollution that now washed around her. They were repulsed by the heavy elements both within and around, a wave of disruption impacting the pattern of the motes' assault on her memories that they had cornered ahead of the final strike.

She was losing her fight with the motes, she knew she had moments before annihilation, she would be consumed by the dying threads of the star or drown in the pollution. Tij had lived her entire existence under the light, in the cohesive form of the star, when the sphere had rules, but this was savage hunger, it was survival.

Tij felt along the memories that had been corralled by the motes. The wave of disruption had brought focus, a realisation of who and what she was. She recognised herself; she was not pain, not grief, she was more than that. This single epiphany led to others, a cascade of awareness, and with it came fury at what was being done to her. Tij had redeemed worlds, brought mercy to those who suffered even when it cost her, all to feed the star to preserve the sphere to ensure continuance, she had never failed in that purpose. Tij refused to suffer anymore.

Anger is a consolation, a distraction, and provided a moment where the agony could not touch her, and in this moment the depths of the pollution spoke to her, cutting through the anguish. She could breathe the pure heavy elements of the pollution, it nourished her, but it was an overwhelming flavour, bitter and metallic, filled with misery and loss so much deeper than hers, concentrated and aged like distilled whisky.

Tij felt the pocket of resistance increasing within her, not communicating in words but cadence, urging the dark pollution to reach further, allowing it to gain strength as the motes still swarmed within her. This was a separation, a distillation of her own, and the influence of the pollution and objects around her. Tij gathered her consciousness, the parts of herself that felt distinct by familiarity, feeling a heavy weight as her thoughts coalesced, chased by both the fetid misery of the pollution and bright starving joy of the motes. There was once again a border within her, drawn by her, a solid recognisable part of her that was purely herself, beyond pain, beyond grief, where she remembered that she was so much more.

Both pollution and instinct inspired. Tij had redeemed the essences of countless people, all their collective memories and experiences, in service to the star. The pollution she lay within held the painful, rejected elements deemed useless to the star, but it had all once been held within her. When Tij redeemed the person, she took everything, the good and the bad, the useful and the broken, it was not her that discriminated based on usefulness, but the engine.

Tij saw in her mind a story that was transmitted by the pollution-drenched objects around her; what was here had been curated.

Tij absorbed the story from the objects around her, pulling it into herself. She could feel the jagged flow of potent unfettered emotion, inspiration that sparked a reaction in her deep memory of all she had known and suffered to lose, the stratification of grief embossed with flecks of joy at having had such proximity to so many joyful things. It was a sullied mix of impure fuel that repelled the motes. Tij could feel each mote release, snapping away from the fuel they did not want. The motes fled from Tij releasing the final coils of the ribbon from the engine, from Tij.

Redemption was a known ritual, but the story of the objects held by the heavy pollution was unlike anything Tij had ever experienced. It behaved in the same way as any other memory she had taken, feeling and thought, pain and joy, it was all the same matter, the same ingredients, its reactions were different, the speed of its flow varied, but it followed the same rules. What was a life after all but a story?

Tij redeemed the story left here, taking it into her using the familiar ritual of redemption, eliciting a response from her subconscious, the redrawing of borders, the distillation of self and purpose. It was a thought that Tij held for a mere second when the bright ribbon the engine was following was suddenly gone and replaced by a deep-red shadow.

Meco watched, transfixed and powerless, as Tij ascended in the engine. She had become entwined in the ribbon of light, the last remnant of the star, which was burrowing into the sphere. Meco felt the tendrils of the robot slide deeper into his flesh as he was held aloft. Through the agony he felt something coil around the pen he still held in his torn pocket and watched in utter confusion and disgust as the robot drew the wire that held his pen back into itself.

Meco cried out, he focused his rage on the robot. His years of experience and skill as a hunter had not prepared him for this, this was not a quarry he had ever faced, he did not know how to defeat it, or if he could, his attack was pure desperation, it was a hopeless state, one he had seen many times when he had hunted the Seeds.

Meco's nostrils were filled with the smell of the thick black oil that covered every part of the robot. With his eyes he traced one of the many tendrils that jutted from the robot to where it pierced his flesh. He shivered, fear juxtaposed by confusion, as he was gently lowered then pinned to the floor by what felt like a full ton of metal.

He could only turn slightly toward Tij, reaching out to her as she disappeared into the air. Tij's face contorted in fear, pressed against the glass walls of the engine, pounding on it with her fists, and she slumped to the floor.

The robot's tendrils, coils of shifting wires, were solid as they held him down, piercing his flesh, creating a thousand new scars, but only causing pain when he moved or tried to fight; this was a surgical application of force. He soon learnt that when he laid still the pain was much less. But this enforced passivity did not sit well with Meco, full of fury and fear at what the robot had just done to Tij and the sight of watching the star disappearing as it crashed into the sphere filled him with manic energy that coursed along nerve and scar.

Contorting himself in helpless struggle, Meco could feel the tendrils of the robot digging deeper, the invasion of cold metal, needle thin shards, forced their way along his spine until they touched the base of his brain, and then he saw in an instant transmission from oil-soaked tendril to raw nerve, the full story of everything the robot had done to make this happen, the meticulous sowing of the objects forcing all the Seeds into a narrow location where the star struck the surface, he saw the effect of what the robot named pollution, the oil that coated it, which was now inside his body.

Meco saw in this transmission what the pollution was, the filtered, heavy thoughts and memories that would not easily burn, and watched the full story play out in his mind showing him the robot and Control becoming infected by all the heavy memories, the fear, misery, despair, helplessness and longing that they filtered out from the harvest, the unwanted pollution of a generation.

'Why?' The word slid out between Meco's gritted teeth. The robot did not move. Meco felt all but one tendril retreat down his spine, the cold of the metal replaced by a warm rush of blood and pain. The sharp tendril was pushed into Meco's mind. He gasped, not from pain this time, the only sensation was one of freezing cold followed not by an image but a flood of data, analysis all showing the same thing: there was not enough fuel, the star was slowly starving, eventually it would sate its hunger by consuming the world and everything in it, this was the inevitable fate of the sphere. Then data twisted into words and whispers of static poured into Meco.

'A system cannot change if it is witnessed, self-preservation will interfere, the system will defend itself – to conserve and protect – the keepers of the system cannot understand that true change is the fruit of cataclysm, that grows from a warped tree whose roots are nourished by the soil of generations passed – the robot must remove all witnesses so the change can grow.'

Meco's subconscious whispered a question: 'Why did hope feel like chaos?' As the final tendril pulled back from Meco's mind, the cold feeling remained.

There was no plan, this was chaos. Meco laughed as he leant in toward the tendrils, the pain fuelling his anger.

'All my life,' he screamed, 'all I know, my job,' Meco's voice broke, 'I did my job. This was all I had, all I am, and you took it away.'

The answer was given in a burst of cold static: 'You will forget, you have always forgotten, soon, all witnesses of the past will be gone, history is habit not purpose, habit does not deserve your loyalty, you will forget this too. When the world is new, then you will be free.'

Meco stared into the fibrous form of the robot that was pinning him in his misery. He began to rock violently from side to side, the response from the robot was to press tendril against nerve. Meco convulsed, smashing scarred fists into coil and tendril. The robot did not fight back, each strike caused a slight separation of the wires pinning his flesh, revealing gaps in the fibrous metallic limbs that eviscerated him. Meco's increasingly desperate movements were causing the coils and wires to reshuffle as they compensated to adjust his restraint. Meco spotted a pattern in the robot's movements, each new shift of form took time to set and balance – an exploitable weakness? He could see objects between the coils that were swept away by grimy tendrils into the robot's depths, strange disparate objects, a cup, a book, the odds and ends of life on the sphere.

Meco's curiosity was only temporary, nothing more than a momentary distraction swept away by the measured focus of his rage. Gritting his teeth, Meco uttered guttural cries in response to the robot's reaction to his struggle. The response was a deeper evisceration, as devastating as it was effortless.

Fear amplifies pain, Meco's flesh and mind were in agony, the world, Tij, everything he knew, his very purpose and existence was as shredded as the star itself. He steeled himself for what would certainly be an end, his final resistance in the face of inevitability.

The robot responded to Meco's struggles in kind; the more he fought the more the tendrils dug into his flesh to restrain him. He would be free, or he would be gone, he would not be held and tortured, forced to watch the world end.

Meco's practised instinct served as a prism, separating feeling from thought, as he analysed his current state. His senses sharpened by desperation, would need direction and purpose, not mindless reaction. He could feel every muscle being pierced in response to his movements, but no bone was broken, no tendon cut, the wires dug deep but with precision, they provided just enough connection to each nerve to maximise agony, but not damage.

Meco was deciding his last action as the shadows changed from a single source fragmenting into a dark web.

The ribbon split as it screamed past overhead. Meco watched it move from a solid, continuous shard to a threaded state, much like the fibrous nature of the robot that held him. Meco saw, through the shifting gaps in the robot, the last of the ribbon, which resembled a web, a web that had firm hold of Tij and the engine.

Despite the pain it caused, he needed to bear witness, every part of him needed to witness the end of light. Meco strained to see between the gaps of the robot as the last of the ribbon, spread wide and thin, caught the remnant of the engine. Meco screamed helplessly as he watched Tij disappear into the surface of the sphere.

# Chapter 11 – Sowing the Darkness.

Tij was helpless, a marionette to the force of velocity, pinned to the roof of the engine, drenched in pollution. The starving motes that had sought to consume her had retreated to the few threads of ribbon that clung to the engine, dragging it down as it hurtled toward the surface. The pollution stung her eyes, her vision smeared like the glass of the engine, each pane of the engine was set starkly against the bright light of the ribbon, like living watercolours, painted in dark shades.

She was just another of the many objects that had broken free of their curated order that was pinned and saturated by force and pollution. The unguent liquid smelled as it tasted, of wet soil and rust, and it was everywhere, washed around the engine as it was thrown around, caught in the grip of the ribbon of light. Terror filled her, juxtaposed by a warped form of elation, a manic gratitude that her heavy grief had been displaced.

Light in the engine switched instantly from searing white to a deep red, the air changed suddenly, causing her ears to pop, the atmosphere felt pressurised, it was thick and dense, the roar of the engine and the vibration triggered by its descent had an alien quality and sounded like it was travelling through water.

An inescapable world had been breached. The ground had always felt so firm beneath her feet but was being cut through by the shredded star as easily as a blade through water, the only evidence of any resistance was the increasing vibrations that shuddered through the engine, screeching as it came into contact with whatever was below the surface of the sphere.

As the screeching increased, filling the air with the sound of tortured metal and glass, the engine was torn from the grasp of the ribbon. Friction caused the engine to slow, while the ribbon relentlessly delved after its quarry. Free of the driving light, the descent abruptly halted. Tij, pollution and all the objects crashed to the floor in a sodden heap.

Tij rose unsteadily to her feet, wading through the ankle-deep pollution, which dripped on her like rain. She walked tentatively toward a pane of glass to the side of one of the ruptured vats, which was now empty. Rubbing her hands across the glass, trying to clean the pollution, was useless, it was too thick. She looked around for something to use, but there was nothing that was not saturated, Tij rubbed her hands on her clothes, but if anything, it sullied her hands even more. She peered through the glass where the pollution was thinnest.

The engine dropped suddenly in momentary free fall. Tij felt the dropping sensation as lines of deep red flashed past the opaque glass. Through the thin gaps between the pollution, she could see the strata that made up the subsurface of the sphere, a mix of soil, rock, and rooms, all warped and contorted by pressure and gravity, twisted into abstract angles. It was from the rooms where the red light flowed.

There was a layer of what looked like crystal; Tij could see that the crystals were interconnected in thick webs of dark-red light.

The engine dropped again Tij lost her footing and slipped to the floor. The pollution was thinning, it was no deeper than the depth of the hand she pushed herself up with. In the thinning pollution there were slight rivulets, each moved toward a pile of objects. Were they absorbing it?

Tij felt the heavy sick feeling return as the engine fell, causing her to slip back to the floor. She felt powerless, lost, there was no way to understand what was happening, she had no frame of reference, no knowledge from an eternity of memory and experience, there was nothing to explain it.

She lay flat on her back, coated in misery, and laughed manically; here at the end of the world there was nothing but baffled echoes and laughter. Is this how it would end? She felt a thrill of excitement course along her nerves.

Splaying her hands beside her, she could see the pollution had been reduced to a mere residue, smeared across the glass and metal. As she lay there contemplating the end a thought came to her: What was beneath her now? Where had the star gone? Spinning around she drew herself to her knees and clawed at the final residue covering the glass beneath, scraping at the dark thick pollution.

Through the glass she could see the final light of the disappearing ribbon as it forged a tunnel beneath her, its bright light now little more than a pixel of intense white far below. The bright light died and was replaced by an angry red of scorched rock and crystal.

Tij placed a protective hand on her stomach, it was an instinctive reaction as excitement warped into fear. This was where all those she had redeemed had rested. At the moment she was on the verge of being consumed by light, the dark pollution-soaked objects had given her a symphony of misery, psalms of desperation and loss that had saved her, redeemed her from being consumed by the rabid motes of the ribbon. A fleeting salvation.

The engine juddered, continuing its sharp, halting descent. Tij could hear the friction as the surface of the tunnel's wall scratched against glass and metal. The vibration sent waves through Tij as it reverberated. She covered her ears; the sound stabbed its way repeatedly into her senses.

Sharp discordant noise cut across Tij's nerves; the stuttering descent was unbearable. The engine slowed once again and Tij began to hear words and melodies, their rhythm dictated by the speed of the descent.

The engine's fall was slowed by a narrowing of the tunnel; the sounds became clearer. Tij felt the vibrations through her feet and hands first and then her whole body became filled with the words and songs pulled from the sound of the engine as it scraped along the tunnel's surface, the passing of the engine like a needle on a record.

Resonance was everywhere, it was bouncing off each surface and object. These were the sounds of the Seeds, she recognised them from many redemptions, their memories always felt heavier and were harder to contain than the Blissed.

Tij could see the red glow of radiant crystal between the twists of wall and soil. She could tell from the sound and feeling that was transmitted from them that these were once Seeds, now crystalised into the solace they built for themselves to shield them from their inevitable fates. The star that they were so desperate to avoid had come crashing down to burn its way into their world, striking them in their maladapted solace, fusing the Seeds and their solace together, linking them all into interconnected strata, all done with a searing stroke of velocity. This is what the star did, converting one element to another.

The vibrations were discordant, even when slowed, there were so many voices talking, telling stories of loss and devotion, singing songs of consolation. There were images threaded through the notes, and when the fall of the engine slowed, they became visible but fleeting, a flicker book offering glimpses, nothing more.

Tij's sanity finally cracked, the thin borders of her mind as scratched and ruptured as much as the glass of the engine. Catastrophe spoke to her, it did not make sense, it was incoherent and terrifying, but these were experiences and memories she had never seen, all hidden from her, from the world, the Seeds they belonged to would have found redemption eventually but not now, not like this.

At home, Tij had kept her own objects, relics from lovers and friends lost, these were the ones special to her that she could not let go, the ones she had hidden away in the dark rooms of her home, suffering for her. She felt selfish, she had not coerced them, they were not prisoners, but Tij refused to give them permission to leave her. She was not the cause of their suffering, but she knew she enabled it, redemption was the only form of release on the sphere, everything else was new or suffering. Surrounding each one of her most beloved she had kept building a version of the solace that the Seeds used, but all she could construct was a thin and brittle constellation.

Each crystal sang with a hundred stories, a thousand images, songs and feelings. When the descent was stable and the rhythm steady their transmissions could be followed easily, one would lead to the other in unexpected ways, but the descent was unpredictable, its uneven journey wove chaotic patterns speaking with myriad voices, it felt simultaneously like discovery and intrusion. So much of what Tij heard was bittersweet with loss and celebration, all resonant testaments of what each Seed had kept or sought.

Tij looked up and back to the world she had left, the routine of it, the certainty, everyone she had known and everything she had done was behind her now.

Tij's reality fell back into focus through the dissonance like a slap in the face; here she was trapped in a glass and metal engine, an engine she had been thrown into, tied to the violent descent of a ribbon of burning light that was once the star to which her life had been entirely devoted.

This star in its new form had tunnelled through matter and life that Tij did not know existed. This tunnel, simultaneously her prison and escape, was singing to her, its notes, its words and rhythms were external, a radiation that trickled down her nerves like caustic rain, sharing gifts as plentiful and relentless as they were brief.

Her fall had brought inspiration, a moment of frenzied respite and reflection, all created from the world ending.

In this moment, the maelstrom turned and Tij was adrift and at peace in the requiem of chaos and consolation around her. When the engine dropped, the cadence of the songs changed, the speed of the descent hastened, as did the contact with the surface of the tunnel. Where everything had been calm for a brief instant, the vibrations were now lurid and screaming.

The resonance that had felt like an embrace was now carving its way through Tij's senses. There was too much. Tij screamed but it was just another vibration lost in the chaos.

Caught again by an unseen narrowing of the tunnel, the engine slowed. The same songs were now deeper in tone, thickened by the density of enforced dysphoria, the sounds and inspirations that only moments ago had driven her to rage and desperation. This new laconic resonance was sickening. Tij felt dizzy, nauseous, and weak, all this potent sensation was causing such polar-opposite feelings and responses, drastic emotional shifts from one to the other, dissonance and dichotomy were nerve shattering, and it was all from the same external source, the vibration caused by the friction between the falling engine and the crystal of the tunnel wall.

Her entire body twisted in revulsion to the depressed rhythm of the engine's descent, as she rolled around convulsing to the terrible discord.

This was torture, as if she was decaying, everything was dissolving. Was she poisoned by the vibrations? Her will, her very self, was soluble, it was terrifying. Tij was once the arbiter of fate and progress for an entire world, a redeemer.

That was the past and it was a single voice, but even recent memory, feelings of joy, revelation and peace, feelings that Tij was certain she had just experienced in her life, became muted by the slowed dysphoric rhythms to the point of blandness. It was as if all flavour, colour and thought were hidden underneath a layer of oily, sickening confusion, all memory that could provide a horizon to focus on, to see or dream a way beyond was lost in this mire. Nothing could break through this suffocating insulation. The violent opposite to what Tij was feeling and experiencing only moments ago now felt alien and unreachable.

The descent changed once more, lifting her slightly from the glass floor. The release from discordant absolute misery was instant, but Tij's senses were still reeling. Yet another slowing brought her crashing to her knees, the rhythm heavy once again but bearable.

Placing her hand down on a pile of objects to steady herself, she pulled her hand away quickly, almost falling over. Her hand was bleeding from a small but deep cut, it was a physical pain serving as an anchor, enabling Tij to focus.

On the pile of objects was a small ceramic swan, it was its broken wing that her hand had found. Reaching down with her wounded hand Tij picked it up, it was just one of the many objects in the engine, but it was the first one she had truly seen; there was a story here, as with all the other objects.

The story of the swan was the simplest thing, it was the briefest recollection of an embrace between her and a green-eyed man, she felt his strong arms around her, their closeness, and the assurance it provided.

Like everything in the engine, it had been placed here just like she had, it seemed so deliberate but how could it be? There was no way of knowing how the tunnel would sing to her, how the impact on the Seeds would turn them to crystal, it was as if meticulous attention was spent on crafting something incredibly intricate and specific only to then throw it into the void in hope.

The engine began to fall again in a bearable descent where the resonance was slow but not excruciatingly so. The discord became a backdrop as Tij looked around the engine, a bubble of glass and metal. Looking up, she could see the top of the tunnel through the thin smear of pollution that was left, but everything was lost in red.

The vibration of her descent continued to sing unfamiliar songs from unheard voices, all telling of familiar emotions and experiences. The sound was swirling around the engine and the pollution-saturated objects. She walked across to the closest pile and placed the broken swan carefully on top.

The objects were all the discarded moments from her life, it seemed impossible, but everything was so familiar. These vital but disposable instances when viewed in isolation could not hold anyone's attention, it was banal, mundane for the most part, but the chaos of the descent was drawing these disparate things together in a melody.

Tij had filled her home with the brilliant and exceptional moments in her life, each relic she cherished was unique and incredible, deemed precious because of its rarity, and these potent moments were the items she had surrounded her lovers with in the solace she had built for them, but in her collection she had neglected the mundane and it was this that made up most of the material of life, it was these trivialities that were the force between the atoms that stopped the world imploding into a hard material, a beautiful material yes, but unwieldy and useless.

Tij saw her life flash through the prism of small moments transmitted from the everyday objects around her. Items worn with use, ignored, and discarded but gathered here. The memories they held filled the air like a thin mist that began mixing with the scent of pollution. Every breath Tij drew filled her with a deep sense of sanctity and sadness.

This new feeling wasn't joy, nothing as ravenous, this was contentment. Suddenly, the weight of grief lifted ever so slightly.

The engine fell again, and the dissonance screamed, but the violent sound was baffled by the warmth and sorrow emanating from the wealth of mundane little moments. It did not stop the pain, it was such poor cloth, but it served as armour to Tij.

It is not only peace that can bring clarity, the world can shred or sink your senses, but it is the space between, where hidden gifts strewn across lives make themselves known. This was a commonplace gift that only wretched circumstance could make precious.

Meco screamed into the frame of the robot as the last of the ribbon that was the star disappeared into the surface of the sphere and everything fell into shadow, then silence; each breath tasted of ash.

The star was gone from the sphere, the darkness felt thick and heavy, all the familiar sounds of the sphere were absent.

The robot, now perfectly still, glistened in the dim reflected embers of a burning world. Meco's senses quickly adjusted to the murk, he could see the fires that were raging around and above him, in forest, field and town.

The air had a sharp metallic tang and was thick with swirling smoke. Meco fell back to the ground, the robot did not adjust its tendrils.

As his eyes adjusted to the new world, Meco could see through the smoke, thick rivers of light, caught by the sphere from the star as it crashed toward its final exit like rags caught on a barbed-wire fence. He watched the Blissed run in their straight lines toward these rivers of light that remained on the sphere; he could see their glowing bodies as dots revealed intermittently through the smoke. The Blissed spread across the sphere and Meco tracked their movements as they formed shifting constellations; the Blissed desperately sought the last scraps of light.

The world was free of the tyranny of the star but not its memory or its legacy, and that legacy played out across the sphere, it was chaos, or hope, call it what you like but the end result is the same. Meco could see the rivers of light where the star had struck the surface and they were scattered all around the sphere, one of these larger rivers was halfway up its concave horizon. He had never been able to see in a straight line across the sphere, the star had been ever present, but now he could see through darkness and smoke to the shreds of light caught in the burning world and the constellations of Blissed that were hunting them.

He had known darkness, he had travelled the dark tunnels in pursuit of the Seeds, but he knew such journeys were a temporary thing, it always felt as if he was holding his breath, able to dive into the dark recesses of the world because he was safe in the knowledge he could return to the surface, back to light to breathe it in once more.

The chaotic world distracted Meco from his plight, he was still, his instincts read the darkness, discerning its character, the look of it, its form was apparent and leering.

Light and darkness were inverted, darkness was master, and the light scurried away, but it was the sound that disturbed Meco most, everything was wrong, it was as if the star that had smashed its way out of the world had taken all clarity with it. Every sound was sporadic and twisted. Loud cracks as wood splintered in flame were wrapped in the cries of the Blissed and ash-drenched wind, all volume ebbed and flowed, each taking a turn to crash against him, the darkness was baffling the sound as it echoed around the sphere.

Meco looked across to the Blissed field, there were a pair of Blissed embracing. He turned to watch, unable to look away as the two of them, still glowing, suffered together, all the other Blissed had fled.

Meco focused on them, and he could see by the way they held one another that they were both incomplete in form, imperfect beings holding each other up, each one having what the other lacked in limb or balance. Meco hated the Blissed and it was hard to reconcile all that he felt with this delicate moment. These two Blissed, raw and new to the shadowy world, awash in memory from the star's brief impact, a fraction of the gift they needed to generate a new form, both undoubtedly starving and terrified, but here they stood, together, in a beautiful defiance of fate. Meco scowled and spat the ash from his mouth. He shivered as a rare cold wind rushed past, his convulsions causing the robot's piercing to dig even deeper to hold him still.

Pain was now a revelation. A body can only hold so much pain and Meco's limit was greater than any other on the sphere, but he was full, there was no escalation beyond what he was feeling right now – physical, emotional, mental – he was full, there was nothing but pain, so there was nothing to hide from.

The robot loomed above him, Meco felt every tendril, cold and sharp, Meco gritted his teeth, the increase in heart rate led to the robot digging deeper into Meco's flesh.

Meco could feel where the tendrils were located, his legs were hardly touched. Bending his knees, he winced as the tendrils around his kidney dug deeper in response. Meco called out for help but then stopped himself, no one would help, they never did.

He fought to rest one foot squarely on the ground. The robot did not respond. Meco pushed his shoulder forward and his arm was placed on the ground beneath him. Meco felt the tendril in the other shoulder pull away,

"End me!" Meco screamed at the twisting morass of wires that was the robot; Meco, now on his knees, grabbed a thick artery of wires with his free hand and pulled the robot toward him. He screamed his pain into its depths, there was no face to look into, no eyes to know, Meco wanted death. Instantaneously, every tendril still piercing his body was retracted, a moment later he saw nothing.

Meco opened his eyes, cold absence replaced pain, his tears betrayed his frustration, the robot did not want him dead. He looked directly at the metal mass looming above him.

The robot had not moved in any direction, but its tendrils were shifting and seething, giving it motion.

Coils of wire slid around each other making the surface of the robot glitter like the carapace of a monstrous beetle. A hole opened at the top of the remaining wire and a pen, wrapped in blood-tipped tendrils, was placed on Meco's chest. The robot scurried away; it was a repellent motion that brought an image of a colossal spider to Meco's mind.

Meco watched the robot scuttle away across the remnants of the Blissed field in a perfect line toward the point where the ribbon that was the star had crashed into the sphere. Easing his way onto his side, the pen slid from his chest onto the floor. Meco could feel fresh new scars begin to bleed all across his body, he held his arms out in front of him, waiting for the healing that always followed. Seconds passed and the blood still ran, he frowned, confused.

Placing both feet on the ground, Meco groaned, lifted himself from the soil and stood upright.

Looking at his feet, Meco could barely distinguish his own shadow among the darkness that was everywhere, he could just make out the pen that the robot had given back to him. Bending down, groaning with ache and age as he did so, Meco picked it up from the floor with one hand and steadied himself with the other.

The image the pen held was familiar, its words once filled with words of consolation now vibrated to the fizzing static of the robot's voice.

'You will forget, you have always forgotten, soon, all witnesses of the past will be gone, history is habit not purpose, habit does not deserve your loyalty, you will forget this too. When the world is new, then you will be free.'

# Chapter 12 – Gravity and Grace.

A longer descent lifted Tij from her feet. There was no sickening feeling this time, no fear, her once ragged breath now steady. Filled with the atmosphere of calm, her subconscious had distilled from the blend of small, forgotten memories held in the objects around her and the residue of pollution that coated everything, reflecting the red light of its oily surface.

The sudden stop was anticipated. She landed on her feet, bending her body into the impact, no longer a slave to the descent. She waited, but the engine did not move.

Tij walked toward the closest pile of objects, it was a collection of souvenirs from her own life, all touched by Tij at some point or held and used by someone she loved, each item incidental, unnoticed in their time together but they were all part of Tij, once forgotten, curated here in the engine.

Standing next to the pile that came up to her waist in a pyramid that had collapsed slightly to her left. It was reminiscent of the residue of life left after the Blissed had all been given redemption, where all that they left behind was treated as junk by a cohort of small machines who cleansed the sphere at the end of every harvest. Clothes, plates, glassware, tools, ornaments, a myriad of things crafted from wood, clay and paint created by those given the gift of creativity, half written journals filled with poems, shoes, music collections, jewellery and photographs, to name but some. Everything that life needed and created, all consequences of existence, taken for granted like the moments that shaped them. What was here in the engine had been gathered from her life, now drenched in the pollution of heavy emotion, the memories they held emitted a palpable atmosphere of sadness around her.

Tij pulled a watch from the pile, though it was still connected by a strand of thick pollution. The face of the watch was cracked, and the rhythm of time was still. She rubbed a thumb over the broken glass. A memory flashed across her mind like a bolt of freezing electricity.

The memory was someone with dark-brown, tear-filled eyes, a shaved head and dark-brown skin covered in yellow tattoos that glowed.

'End it, enough, I've had enough.' With those final strained words, they started to cut across their arms with a knife. Tij rushed forward, swatted the knife free, and held them in a hard embrace. The fresh scars healed under the light of the star and the watch fell from a slim blood-streaked wrist. Kai, their name was Kai.

Carefully placing the watch back, Tij's hand brushed the pile, causing disembodied thoughts to scream across her mind. Each one was a lover or friend desperately lost in agony, pleading, and begging with Tij to release them from a life that they had together. Each face and plea caused her heart to sink further until there was nothing but loss causing her to shiver in the engine tenuously held above the void.

Digging through the pile, Tij let every splinter of memory explode within her, determined to make herself suffer. The eviscerating grief, matched by sharp edges of broken objects, a manic need to hurt herself, to be consumed, it was too much.

Deeper and deeper into the souvenirs. The first few layers were nothing but guilt and sadness, all images, and sensations of the end of a life, a life she had to take.

Her bleeding hand touched one of the objects deeper down. Her fingers curled around an empty wine bottle, and she felt the embrace of strong arms, the laughter they shared echoing through her body as he held her close from behind. She felt his skin, which had started to glow when they woke together that morning. He spun her around and kissed her deeply.

'This life has been all you.' He spoke in a deep voice, smiling through a bearded face. 'Since I woke in this form, there you were, from the first moment to the last second, I loved you, thank you for our time together.'

His name was Sam, and his heartfelt words were interrupted by Tij hitting him with a pillow so he couldn't see her cry.

Slower now, she dug through layers where memories were filled with tactile warmth, laughter, kisses, gentle embraces and passion. Her hands slowed as she revelled in sensory moments; all these people were gone, but here were the memories of the time they'd had together, grief held in balance with gratitude.

Deeper still were the first moments, the awkward introductions, and long meaningful glances. Tij grabbed and pulled a broken wooden carving of an oak tree, snapped along its length, nothing more than a large splinter, drenched in the thick pollution, which gave a deep profundity to this collection of memories of those she first met, those she would fall in love with, knowing the cost, and what would inevitably follow.

This memory was broken, but still potent, in it Tij was sitting, waiting at the base of an oak, blinking in the starlight. Ali dived into the fallen leaves next to her, she had tripped on a root dropping the gift she carried which broke in two. In the memory, Tij picked up one half of the carving, the same one she held in her hands right now, passing the other to Ali who opened her mouth to speak, but here the memory ended.

Tij's grief now had a companion, a chorus of beautiful moments, together they were a dreaming storm of whispers enclosing her in a constellation.

Removing her hands from the pile, Tij grabbed a red shirt, torn through use and being dragged across the sharp edges of broken objects by each descent of the engine. She pulled, carefully easing it free from its entanglement. The material was replete with memory, like everything here, it carried a scent of someone lost to her, the memory was weak but still connected Tij to a moment when a dark-haired woman, wearing the red shirt, sat on a chair with her back to Tij, turning at her approach, her skin glowing, tears in her eyes and the request for redemption on her lips.

Tij kissed the shirt and then tore it into strips to form a bandage. She looked at her hand as it continued to bleed, blood trickling down her fingers. The wound was small but deep and Tij stared at the separation of flesh. The wound was in the same place as one inflicted by Enid; there were no old scars, they were all healed by the light of the star, but this scar would stay.

Wrapping her hand tightly with scraps of the torn shirt, Tij crumpled what was left and walked to the centre of the engine, a flat area in the curve of glass and metal.

Easing to her knees, Tij scraped the thick residue of pollution. She could not be certain if it was the pollution or a sudden epiphany; this was the first action she had taken since being thrown in the engine that was focused on where she was going, not where she was or where she had come from, but her future.

A deep breath eased Tij, the hand she cleared the pollution with was shaking slightly. Balling the hand into a fist, she leant forward, using her forearm to clear more of the pollution away. There was now nothing but a smear between her and the glass.

Tij used the memory-soaked shirt, now rendered into bandage and cloth, to clean the glass below her. The last layer of pollution was gossamer thin and smeared across the glass. Gritting her teeth and groaning in frustration, she held the ripped shirt in both hands and scrubbed frenetically. The memory in the shirt became more potent as it absorbed the heavy elements in the pollution. Tij began to sob, the dark-haired woman, Sara, sat on the chair wearing the red shirt. Her skin glowing, she turned around to face Tij.

'Please,' was all she said.

Tij threw the saturated shirt behind her and felt the calm return with every breath. The mix of memory and heavy element in its concentrated form was potent and visceral.

Through the nearly clear glass, Tij could see her destination, her fate. Beneath her was a vast nothing. Shocked, she looked around through the dirty glass walls of the engine and could see the angry red of the tunnel forcing its way through, she was at the end. Tij blinked in confusion, a cold dread trickled down her spine and she shivered with fear, but it was a fear tinged with excitement.

Rubbing her eyes, as if reality itself could be reset by such a simple act, Tij squeezed her eyes shut tight, breathed the air in three deep breaths and then looked below her. On the other side of the glass was total darkness.

Under the unrelenting light of the star, darkness had been a luxury, a solace. What was before her was a colossal emptiness. Her eyes became accustomed to the void. She could see the ribbon of the star as it stretched out away from her, like a white thread lost in deep velvet. Tij was shaken at just how small light had become. The star had been everything, both tyrant and saviour to the sphere and all that existed in it. Within the ravenous light, it once held all the thought and memory of a world, and here it was, coiled around its prey, bright but distant; it was so small. Everything she had ever known was so small.

Tij lowered herself closer to the glass and was just about to press her face against it when she saw herself in stark relief. The darkness below and the red light around and above had brought her reflection into view. Putting both hands on the glass as if to grab herself, Tij did not recognise what she saw – filthy, blood smeared, her clothes torn and soaked, but it was her expression. What she had felt was her heart racing as she breathed the calming atmosphere, but what she saw was the look of someone insane. Her face twitched around a lost smile, which when her eyes met her reflection turned into a menacing snarl, her eyes were empty, not gone, just bereft of any spark. Tij collapsed to the floor, her breath frosting the glass, ebbing and flowing as she lay prostrate across the glass surface. The thick taste of soil and rust made her retch.

Tij felt the cold glass on her face and her focus narrowed from her reflection to the distant coiled ribbons of light, shifting and convulsing around their prey.

She could see nothing of Control but knew it must still be there, it must be at the centre, it had always been the centre. With a shiver of grief, Tij wondered if Enid was still there, at the centre of the ravenous knot of light, lost in the darkness. Was Enid aware of anything? Could she feel? Was she afraid?

Tij's thoughts were falling back into place, like dust settling after a storm. The descent had changed her, its song was a burst of radiation that she could still feel transmitted by the crystal of the tunnel, a purified and magnified scream of consolation transmitted through the pollution and the curated objects of Tij's that vibrated with its resonance. Everything in the engine was a catastrophic alignment of impossible things, an alloy formed from what survived and what was saved, all tempered into a warped and new precious element.

Once the world surrounded the star, as Tij had surrounded Enid, and now the darkness, the deep void, surrounded the ribbon's shifting threads, trapped in the diminishing orbit of its greed, each thread striking at the centre of the morass. It looked like a thousand bright snakes, coiling around one another, utterly intent on the same prey.

The threads coalesced and reformed over again constantly shifting, trying to find a better way to get to Control to rip it apart and finally sate its hunger. Tij watched the coil's shifting shape, expanding and contracting like the exposed ribcage of a great beast. The shape kept changing, occasionally settling on a form that was a parody of the star it once was. It looked very much like the burnt-out remnant of a house, the walls long since reduced to ash, the structure still intact but ablaze.

The knotted ribbon was the only light Tij could see outside the engine. She looked furtively for her reflection, but there was nothing there, her eyes had adjusted and moved beyond the scope of what she could see before. The ribbon, for all its luminescence, became distant and small, it scorched like a magnesium flare dominating her sight, burning an image on her retinas, making it impossible to see anything else. The ribbon was made caustically bright by the chase and finally the ribbon's capture of its meal.

Tij laughed grimly, her god, her light, the star that was both saviour and tyrant had in the end been so easily tricked. This impossibly dominant thing, the core of a world, was so intent on its greed that even now as it consumed Control, it showed no indication that it was even partly aware that it had been led into the void, fooled like the reckless predator it was.

Something struck the engine from the darkness; the sound was clear and true cutting through the thick atmosphere of the engine, chiming along her every nerve that felt ice-cold.

Tij arched her back, her hands splayed in shock. The alien note echoed around the engine briefly before being absorbed by the pollution. Silence, then a crack that she could feel resonate through the glass beneath her feet.

Tij raised herself onto the balls of her feet, it was instinctive, a vestigial reflex and useless, she was helpless.

Looking around she could not see anything, then the glass was struck once more from the void, then again, each time the glass was struck the resonance changed, like the sound of a snare drum that had been pierced, switching the sound from sharp to flat.

Tij still could not see anything on the glass, everywhere she looked the burning frame of the star remained etched onto her sight like an eye worm. Robbed of one sense, Tij pressed her ear to the glass, she could hear nothing, but she could feel the vibrations that continued in weaker smaller chords, but from what?

Turning her head, looking out into the void, she lined up her scorched retina to match the burning skeleton of the star. She soon realised that the impacts had a rhythm, each was in response to the beating frame of the star. When it expanded, the glass crackled and shuddered.

There was something between the star and her, a presence that pushed against the glass, it spread toward Tij repelled by the new bright ravenous knot of ribbon, beating like a heart in its midst. The glass beneath Tij cracked in response to the darkness pressing against it bringing the notion of a solid emptiness from reverie into quantifiable reality.

Darkness had been a solace to Tij, it was an abyss, a great emptiness, an absence, but this darkness had a character of its own and it was radiating jealousy, she could feel it calling through the glass. Darkness was a solace to itself as if it could only reconcile its own nature when it only had itself to compare it to, but now there was light, a blazing corruption that had been forced upon the void, and when there is light darkness can only ever be its shadow.

Before Tij was an inversion of the world she had served, not in structure, but in hierarchy. Here, as in the world she had known, the light naturally gravitated toward the centre of the void as it was within the sphere, but it was the scale that set it apart. The star had dominated the sphere, its presence made more profound because it was essential to continuance, and all who lived below it knew they were tied inexorably to that truth. All gone now, the light at the centre was an unwanted invader, disrupting the dreaming void.

It was the first time since the robot had thrown her into the engine that Tij's thoughts were for the world. What was the sphere now, was it dark? How could it not be. All the light that she knew to exist now floated out in the void in front of her very eyes. It was one thing being on the edge of a bright world facing the darkness, a barrier between the void and home, but it was a different thing entirely to be the pivot between a new darkness and the old. Would they reach out for one another and would Tij be crushed in between?

Tij knew this is how redemption worked, it drew you in with the promise of renewal. People always sought permission before they became something else, and in the invading light, darkness had a character forced upon it and with it a need, redemption was only ever a beginning. But what Tij did not know was the state of the world behind her.

Looking up, Tij felt a cold shard of relief as the smeared glass above revealed nothing but glowing red light. The world was burning behind her, or was it the crystal still glowing from the impact? Would this be the last light, a dying ember buried between sphere and void? Was the world irreparably scarred by the star's flailing escape, burnt from the reckless greed of the star, or was it caught in the red glow of the Seed crystal? Either way, at least the world was not dark.

She imagined she could see a way clear back to the sphere. Above her was the tunnel but it was still glowing hot, she thought she could see where it ended, but the route back to the sphere was lost in red. Tij knew this light would continue to diminish over time, it would cool then dim and then the darkness of the world would reach out to the void, and they would meet right where she stood.

Could Tij climb, drag her way back to the world? No, the tunnel above was not dug it was forged. She could see through the glass of the engine either side of her, the surface of the crystal tunnel was not perfectly smooth but split by deep cracks, a frame, which strongly suggested a stained-glass window, but the only colour was red. The surface of the tunnel reflected as much as it emitted. Was this the fate of the world above, the sphere split between fear and embers?

The engine slipped once more, dropping a little further. The surface of the tunnel, still molten in places, was not holding the engine firm. This engine had orbited the star, it had resisted its heat and light even as it served its continuance, and its resistance was still evident; at least some things endured.

Even if Tij could climb her way from the tunnel, how could she escape the engine? Any ascent would need her to strike the glass, causing resonance that would prompt a collapse of brittle crystal, and the surface of the tunnel was hot, the air in the engine told her that. The cracks in the tunnel were the only handhold, the only blemish in its structure that could offer any hope of ascent, but the newly formed glass was razor-sharp and brittle. The toll for escape was beyond Tij, and unwanted, so she turned once more to face the darkness.

In the void Tij watched, transfixed by the undulations of the burning skeleton of the star, each shift in movement could be felt as well as seen, echoing through flesh and bone glass and metal alike. The shape of the light narrowed, and the skeleton shifted, its ribs pointing toward her as they convulsed. Was it still feeding? This was the last of Control as it finally collapsed beneath the ravenous onslaught. Tij closed her eyes, the last light in the void burnt onto them and scorched into retina and memory alike, still shifting and breathing.

She opened her eyes when another impact hit the glass beneath her, it lifted her and everything in the engine into the air and Tij landed heavily.

Turning to lie on her side, Tij could barely breathe, winded by the impact, spitting blood from her mouth where she had bit her tongue. She watched the blood as it moved toward a slight crack on the surface of the glass at the exact point of the impact that threw her into the air.

Peering at the hairline fracture in the glass below her, Tij could see a sliver of blackened metal that had penetrated through. This was from Control, she could feel it, the last remnant of what once ruled the world and the architect of its destruction. Tij tentatively reached out her index finger and gently touched the tip of the sliver of metal. She shuddered, the shock caused her to convulse, wincing as the last moments of Control were stabbed into her mind.

# Chapter 13 – Wisdom is Hollow Validation.

Purpose is the opposite of wisdom. Wisdom is a hollow validation used to justify whatever path you wish to travel or wish to avoid. This is the deceit. If you become burdened and harrowed on a particular course you will find wise words of validation, tender notions or scouring edicts to provide comfort and encouragement that you are on the right path, driving you to endure, providing the speaker of these words with a crowd, you become their fuel, ensuring parasitic continuance.

A different path, in the opposite direction, will also bring wisdom scuttling out toward you from the cracks of the world, each with its own tender notions and scouring edicts, its own prophets and tellers, all casting the net of their words to capture you into submission to their realities. Fuel for their ascendance.

When each compass point has the same reward, the same demands, then there is no one true path, there is no wisdom, only purpose. Realising this is what makes you free, it is a sombre truth that most people must read in the scars of their experience that purpose is pure because purpose is both felt and lived. Wisdom is just a borrowed myth.

To Meco, wisdom was a consequence of life, a cumulation gathered by the journey, like mud collecting on a boot. Copious wisdom sits on every direction of travel in all its forms, so how can there only be a single direction? A single truth? Wisdom was as hollow as the world itself. Purpose was pure, it required an aggregation of dissonant things. Killing an animal beyond healing was merciful, breaking a Seed's cocoon and dragging it toward redemption saved the world. Meco did not hold a life within him, he was not a person, he knew this, this was his sacrifice, he was purpose driven by the promise of borrowed dreams. Purpose is instinct, it is his only gift, and every fibre of him crafted by time to serve it, it was duty, it gave him meaning, and this was all Meco had known.

Meco was still holding the pen, listening over and over to the corrupted psalm of purpose and how it had been changed by the robot.

'You will forget, you have always forgotten, soon all witnesses of the past will be gone, history is habit not purpose, habit does not deserve your loyalty, you will forget this too ... when the world is new, then you will be free.' Meco listened to the message over and over, 'Then you will be free'.

Meco could remember that the message in the pen had been changed, but he already could not remember what the original message was, he could recall the feeling of consolation it gave, but not a single scrap of memory remained of what it said.

Every muscle in his body was tense, still swollen and bleeding from the robot's assault. Meco's jaw was clamped tightly shut and he ground his teeth each time he heard, 'Then you will be free.'

'Free, to do what?' He sneered, opening his arms in exasperation.

The only answer was a gust of wind, stinking of the ashes from the burning world. Meco snapped the pen and let it fall from his hand. He looked around at the world through stinging eyes, it was specks of light and trails of fire in the darkness. His other senses came to the fore, he could hear birds' overhead screeching. The air that rushed around him was so much colder than he was used to, raising the hairs on his arms and neck.

Meco stood, staring after the scuttling robot, its path was a direct line to the impact site that took it straight past where Meco last called home.

The thought of home left him cold; home was the reward at the end of his work, a gift to himself for a job finished where he could rest and dream, but now the thought of it felt like a trap, a hole to hide in and drown in uselessness. He did not want to see it, but the robots trail led straight past it and Meco will follow.

He pressed his wounds, each in turn, the pain a reminder to himself that he still felt something other than anger and loss.

He caught sight of the robot and watched it disappear into the swirling smoke and darkness of a dark wood, but he knew the direction it was taking was as straight as purpose, and it led to the red wound in the surface of the sphere inflicted when light escaped the world.

Meco felt heavy, exhausted, he would have healed under the light of the star but now his body stayed as broken as the world. Putting one foot in front of the other, he began to walk, slowly at first as his wounds continued to weep. He soon reached the edge of the Blissed field, which was so much dimmer in the world without a star; it reflected the reality of the burning sphere. On its surface Meco could see the fires had spread across town and field, forest and factory, and dancing in between were the wandering constellations, the specks of light that were the Blissed as they fled, desperate and hungry across the sphere, hunting the last shreds of light, to consume and escape.

A thin layer of ash lay over everything, it was falling like snow. Meco found himself hoping for the world to be buried, but unlike the Seeds he once hunted, neither he nor the Blissed would have built any solace for themselves.

Lost, he felt panic for the first time. Fear he knew, it was an old friend, but this was a juddering dread that caused his ruined body to shake, wringing every last bit of pain from his eviscerated muscles and flesh. Subconsciously, he reached for the pen, the panic rose like a firework up through his nerves, exploding in his brain – gone, everything was gone.

'You will be free,' Meco repeated the words. Anger reignited the wreckage of his purpose, he knew what he needed to do, he would track the robot, it was a splinter of purpose and Meco needed a reason to put one foot in front of the other, there was nothing else.

The darkness sat upon the surface of the world like ill-fitting clothing, a heavy material, thick with searing threads of fire and light swept through it. All the occupants of the sphere were fleeing, a herd of deer ran past him, smashing into branches in a reckless bid to escape the world. Above him, Meco could hear a colony of birds screeching overhead, their calls mingling with the screams of the Blissed who ran loose, still molten, setting anything they touched aflame. Nature was fleeing ahead of them, torn between a fear of this new darkness and the danger posed by light and the fire it brought, it was a corruption of instinct; fight or flight were no longer opposite points on the compass,

Meco was gathering data, beginning to understand the rules of this new world, looking for patterns he could predict, understanding was only useful to him as far as it served his purpose, it was a vestigial habit.

He could see nature itself flee from the sources of light around him, committing itself to hiding in the thin border of shadow that surrounded it, but never straying too far. He could hear life all around him through the chaos, as they hid in the hinterland of shadows, unwilling to trust absolute darkness but terrified of the light. They neither ate nor drank but existed in a state of terror, nourished by fear; it was thin gruel, and they would soon starve.

Following the tracks left by the robot, even in virtual darkness, was a simple task. Its tendrils tore through the ground, ploughing its way forward. The path of the robot was direct, taking it past Meco's home, following the line of travel. Meco could see one of the rivers of light, the scraps from the star lay across the trail ahead, which was through the woodland that ran along the edge of the road at the sphere's equator. The darkness here was mitigated by a thinning canopy of flames, and Meco could finally see the path clearly, this direction would take him home.

Meco paused once more. What had become of Tij? Where had the star taken her? He looked at the ground beneath his feet and just for a second wondered if he could feel vibrations from the star below.

Meco shook his head, wherever Tij was it was beyond his understanding. Guilt crept into his mind, could he have done more?

All Meco knew was gleaned from practice, instincts honed by repetition, his only excuse was that he was pinned by the robot, but the truth was no comfort.

Peering ahead through the smoke-heavy woods, Meco saw through the shifting tunnels formed between fire and smoke. Meco knew the strangeness of what he saw, the shadows were all wrong, its source was from the surface upward, this was another inversion of the world as it once was, it was of no consequence; This was one of the rivers of light.

The world was monotone, details on the plants and trees around him were thrown into stark relief by the source of light, which was growing brighter as he approached through the trees.

Meco soundlessly pushed through low hanging branches to a clearing. The light glowed ahead of him lighting the sphere from the ground upwards. All around him were long gap-toothed shadows thrown by the trees, he noticed they were all pointing in slightly different directions, one pointed right at him, this was a length of temporary darkness made possible by light and it laid a path on the ground for him to follow.

A scream erupted behind him, shocking him into action. He dived to the side, and away, landing heavily on a clump of ferns. He twisted his head around as he landed to see a molten Blissed, still person-shaped from the waist down but in shreds above. Each one of these extremities bore the remnants of a face and all of them were screaming, it did not even pause to look down on Meco. The torn Blissed ran forward, clumsily crashing through the ferns, shrubs and trees, everything it touched was burning, the flames stealing darkness from the shadows they clumsily wore.

Meco saw another Blissed just through the woods to his left, over a slight incline of the wood's floor. This Blissed was not screaming, it was gelatinous, there was no discernible features that he could see, its silent procession was no less frenzied as it followed the shredded Blissed leaving the same flame and chaos in its wake.

The animals were no longer silent, the rampaging Blissed put the birds to flight and unseen mammals ran off in panic away from the flames. Nature usually spoke of patterns and rhythms all familiar to him, but now he was listening to the splintered patterns of chaos, the lack of order frayed his nerves.

Meco cautiously continued to follow the trail through the woods, creeping forward, easing himself around the burning path that followed the Blissed in their wake. He focused on the sounds and smells around him, the strange echoes and resonance caused by all the stricken life in his proximity. Everything he heard and felt of the world was fear and desperation, it all felt brittle and hollow, even the resolute ground he stood upon bore the unprecedented burdens of ash and flame along with the weight of strange shadows, which sat so poorly on the frame of the world.

Ash-filled gusts swept around him, all in opposition to each other, a vortex of wind, more evidence that the air itself was just as lost as the broken world. The wind fanned the flames littered on the woodland floor, lifting a colony of motes skyward, creating brief constellations, which Meco passed through as he continued forward.

The wood ahead was on a slight incline. The air, already hot and dense with ash carried shrill, screeching and unintelligible cries, which he judged were co-located with the source of light that threw a smoke-fused wall of light just past the summit.

He knew the approximate distance; he could guess the source of the sounds and they lay just past the line of trees at the top of the incline. He grasped the bark of a crooked tree, which would serve as the last support before reaching the summit and looked behind him.

He could see the edge of the Blissed field, almost covered in a blanket of ash, now only reflecting the world in random gaps revealing the polished past, showing the temporary clarity of fire and constellations.

The shadows of his immediate vicinity were projected on the world behind him. These shadows were all laid like corpses upon the ground, fractured and merging where they fell on one another, and among them he could see his own shadow, it was greater in scale and depth than it ever had been under the star.

Grabbing bracken to lift himself the final distance he stood at the top looking down into a miasma of piercing light, and as his eyes fought to adjust, the wind, laced with cacophonies of sound, was thrown into his face. The light was less than the star, but in the new darkness every scrap was a feast, and here the Blissed were feeding.

Meco knew this place. Holding his hand in front of his eyes he looked for his home, which once sat at the top of a small hill, as far from life as he could get. The river of light was a savage wound that bit deep into the sphere's surface. As silently as he could, Meco stayed on the ridge, resting on the trees for support. He could then see the remnants of where he once lived at the very edge of the river of light, where the ribbons of the star first scratched into the ground.

Stepping down toward the ruin, Meco found himself running toward what was left of where he lived, so little of the world belonged to him, all he had was here scattered along the bright shore of the river. Meco's home was little more than a small collection of rooms that poked their way through the surface of the sphere, made of brick and carved stone that lay in a trail of destruction in front of him. Every stone and beam were shattered, all that remained above knee height was a corner of one of the rooms where the soil was thickest.

The river began where his home ended. Meco put his back to one of the few standing walls and leant against it heavily.

The pain from a wound does not come from the void in the flesh, it comes from the area around the separation, not where the blood rises to replace the flesh that is torn away but the sudden edge, now a severed border, the wall of flesh that had met the blade that it could not resist, it could only yield.

Meco looked across the river of light that flowed away from him. The scene ahead became seared into his vision, first in scratches of shadow, then layer upon layer built up.

The river, one of the remnants of the star, trapped by the ragged edges of the world, was a scar on the surface of the sphere, not filled with blood but with light, an open wound, a swathe of devastation made stark by the brilliance of it, light set against the dark and smouldering ash of the shore that surrounded it. It was this very luminescence that was calling to the Blissed, who were running into it recklessly. It was a curved river, thousands of paces long, tapered at each edge. Meco saw that none of the Blissed within this bright water were emersed beyond chest height.

All light is a consequence of reaction, the star itself had burnt memories to light and heat the world, and here in this bright water were the remnants of that process, but it was dying, the memories that flowed around it could not be replenished.

The light of the star itself was a consequence of old elements being shattered and fused into something new, this was what lit the world, the rivers of light were isolated, hunted, and vulnerable, it was only a matter of time before it would darken, no new fuel would come, there would be no motion or collision to create new elements to burn. The world was haunted by the light it used to serve.

The Blissed that waded through the bright water were all feeding as they wallowed in the shallow light, each was becoming a new thing, a new shape, a new life, all taken from the memories and experience that were held in the light. The Blissed were consuming relentlessly until their forms were complete.

Meco watched as they shifted through phases of being, morphing from the rabid broken shapes that he had seen crashing through the wood to get here where they and all the other Blissed were busy consuming the light like parasites.

Meco knew the process, he had seen it so many times, but this time it held a fascination he'd never felt before. The light here was finite, the Blissed were oblivious to this fact, or they didn't care, driven as they were by desperate hunger, each of the Blissed were greedily consuming the light, turning the memories it held into new forms, that shape was always unknown, the memories and experience they hungered for dictated who they would become. This would be the last forge, here their shapes were cast, and the light would be consumed until finally the Blissed were no longer the torn and shredded beings that moments ago were crashing their way through woods and towns.

The Blissed were reborn, satiated recipients of the promised gift of renewal and the forms and experiences they now wore.

A settled consciousness followed the settled form, they were new to themselves, each held memories and knowledge, was new and unknown to them and all the experience they contained was from a world that was gone. Meco could see the Blissed in this the final phase of their transformation, first the form then personality, emotion followed, this was the connecting tissue of any living thing, binding it to the world.

Meco continued to watch with sneering gratification, as the relief of their new forms turned into fear of an unknown world that was burning.

# Chapter 14 – The Void is a Lens.

With her index finger on the shard that pierced the glass of the engine, Tij absorbed the death of Control, its last moments out in the unknown void, finally ripped apart by the ravenous light.

Tij shuddered as she felt the story of Control transfer from the shard, another life given redemption. She winced, the essence of someone she gave redemption to was a fluid thing, this was data drenched in emotion, it felt cold and sharp like broken glass in freezing water, it was a relentless transmission that crawled along her nerves to her brain.

The image in Tij's head was of a perfect silver metal sphere, where the cracks were bleeding thick, deep-red fluid. The dissonance of metal and thought was palpable and beat a frenetic discordant rhythm inside her chest, it was torture, red-hot emotion then ice-cold logic. Tij felt her mind crack at the onslaught. She tried to pull away her finger from the shard, she paused, in its last moment Control was afraid.

Fear poured through the connection, then agony as Tij absorbed the story, up to the final chapter where Control was torn apart by the ravenous light. Tij felt a rush of sympathy, which became lost in a flash of anger. The light was not chasing Control, it was chasing the harvest it held. In that collected fuel, filtered of heavy elements, was her lover, her friends, a part of everyone she knew, each and every one of them she had given redemption, where they were all torn apart.

Tij felt the story of Control wash through her mind, cold metal and hot emotion telling how Control and the robot had become polluted by what they had filtered from the harvest, how they had become affected by it, the catalyst of their corruption.

In Control's story was a solitary thought for the robot, it was the merest flicker, dissonance of gratitude and resentment for how it had become corrupted. A manic sadness that caused Tij to laugh, it was only when she tasted tears that she realised she was crying.

Control removed itself from the system to preserve it.

Control cannot precede chaos, for as long as it exists Control will seek to balance and enable. It must remove itself from the system to ensure the survival of the sphere. Tij's head was filled with numbers and formulae, all counting down to zero.

Tij spoke out the final words as they were transmitted to her:

'Control was the system, it is all we have ever known, it is the tyranny of balance. The system removed itself from the equation, not out of certainty for the future, but to enable it.'

The remnants of Control peppered the surface of the glass, causing Tij to reflexively pull her hand away from the shard. She watched through tears as each impact penetrated the glass of the engine, hairline cracks were spreading like a web across the glass, each crack caused Tij to cringe.

There was nowhere to go. Tij looked around in panic, her heart pounding, striking every taught sinew in deep discordant chords. The engine was mostly glass, her inevitable fate was crystal clear.

Defeated, Tij knelt on the glass to face the void, she could see below her the ribbons of the star still wrapped in a tight, squirming knot around what was left of Control. She could not tell if the star was smaller, since it had reformed outside of the sphere. The star was so far away it was impossible to tell.

Tij had always sought the darkness, it was a solace where she slept and dreamt. These had been precious, selfish moments in her long life in service to the star's tyranny. She stared into the void as it pressed against the cracking glass and wondered if it would let her dream.

Looking around through the dust-filled air at the piles of curated, pollution-drenched souvenirs from her life, Tij felt afraid, but not alone.

The dust danced through the red light in chaotic whorls and eddies, everything held a partial significance that changed through interaction or observation. Tij was seeing logic in the chaos.

The air held more than dust, it resonated to alien sounds: the crackling of the tunnel's surface as it cooled above, the splintering of the glass beneath her knees.

Exhausted, Tij lay face down on the glass, it felt cool as it carried the vibration of every crack and split.

Closing her eyes, Tij heard whispering, not words but cadence, a mix of sighs and the drawing of breath, it was barely perceptible, but it was there. It was the void, and it was speaking. Such an idea felt ludicrous,

The engine vibrated to the sound of loud cracks and the chime of glass scraping crystal. The sides of the engine were the instrument of resonance, it was the sound of connection as its glass and metal touched the cooling sides of the tunnel.

Tij fell, a few seconds of free fall followed, until the tunnel narrowed and caught hold. She fell hard onto the glass floor. The impact lessened because she didn't fight it, the descent was inevitable, she felt a smile spread across her face through the fear – she was ready.

Again, she heard whispering, barely coherent, coming in waves, but waves were made of something, water, or sound, it was tangible. There was only one conclusion: the void was not empty. Tij could hear it lapping against the window of the engine.

Drawn toward the whispering void, Tij felt the story she had absorbed from the pollution-soaked souvenirs, the story that had saved her from the starving motes, was reaching out to the void.

Looking around at the souvenirs on the piles facing her, Tij felt a hook of familiarity grabbing her eye and then drawing her mind toward the memories held there. A collection of small but poignant things, but what Tij kept in her home were the shining testaments of life, the big events, the loud and profound, it occurred to her that in chasing joy she had neglected all the times she had been content.

Was this everything, she wondered? No, it could not be, there wasn't enough to cover the full extent of Tij's long life, which meant once again that what was here was curated. Walking around the mounds of items from her life, Tij let the hooks of memory ensnare her and take her mind back to a beautifully simple moment. Running her hands across the collection to her left, Tij looked at each of the objects as they fell: a watch, a mug and then a book. Tij frowned, the book was not hers. Leaning down, she picked it up. Bound in dark-red leather, dripping wet and torn, its spine broken, it was completely unreadable, but it showed her a story.

She saw the robot, scuttling across the engine toward a heap of discarded and broken wooden items. It took its time selecting a red book. In a chorus of stolen voices, sound emanated from the robot, it was not speech, it was a transmission. Each voice overlapped; all were known to Tij but before she could fully recollect them the voices had changed and spoke directly to her.

'The harvest was failing, there was not enough.' The words were awkward, threaded together from moments out of context. A flicker book of images, graphs, and reports too quick to be seen but voices here told her in a single sentence what took the robot so long to realise: 'The harvest was failing, the star would consume everything, all would be lost.'

'We did not know.' The tone of the voices lowered. 'We all maintain the sphere as it is, we are devoted to its continuance.' Tij felt a shiver creep up her spine, the voices continued, lowering to a reluctant tone, as if ashamed. 'We must all be removed, the future is not ours to give because we cannot dream, we can only know.' Tij let the book drop but holding on with thumb and forefinger. 'The future will not need redemption, this is our gift to you, all that you have forgotten, returned, so you can dream.' Tij shook her head as the last words were transmitted: 'Be free.'

Tij gasped for breath, this was not a gift, this was a prison of memories. She threw the book, hearing it thud dully against the glass. She could feel the weight of the void pressing against the splintering engine, she could hear the whispers of the void as the waves hit the engine, each impact causing the cracks in the glass to rush further across the surface.

It was a prison that had taken her out of the world. In the face of the void the anger fell away from her, fear, grief, it all fell away, it was useless armour she no longer wanted, she would welcome what was to come.

Tij was ready, comforted by the pollution and relics of her life, she was manipulated by whatever had curated them, but this is all inspiration truly is. There was no sense of threat from the life around her, or the story still held within, even as her heart raced adjacent to it.

The story was a reliquary of every moment she had forgotten. Despite being adrift in the engine, sitting at the edge of the void, Tij felt at peace with herself, and her place at the crossroads of this new reality, the void was unknown, terrifying, and relentless, it was testament to the story she had redeemed from the lost moments of her life, and the success of their manipulation that chaos brought solace.

Tij, hanging from a burning world, battered by the waves of the void, scarred by grief, was lost in reverie of the small, lost moments of her life. Such was her peace she did not even notice as the engine dropped from the world and drifted out into the void.

Floating in darkness Tij reached out her arms and legs, her fingers brushed against something cold and metallic, a spark flashed briefly between the object and Tij's index finger and at that moment it transmitted a memory.

A sudden sense of warmth poured across Tij's skin, and then light, causing her to squint. She raised her hand in front of her face, but the hand was not hers, it was large, strong and glowing a dull red. The memory took hold and Tij felt herself pour into the scene and the body that was sitting in a meadow full of white and yellow flowers all looking directly up at the star above them.

The light and heat intensified, every one of Tij's nerves felt like it was on fire. The man she was now grabbed a handful of grass and ripped up clumps mumbling incoherently while he did so. He looked up at the star and Tij felt his hatred, like a ball of electricity throbbing in his head, matching his racing heart. He looked across the concave horizon and Tij recognised her home. He stood and ran toward it, and then the memory was gone. Tij was back in darkness, she breathed in deeply and exhaled. Her eyes strained, trying to adjust, she could just about see the faint ember of red as the tunnel to the world appeared above her. She must be spinning, all the objects filled with her forgotten memories were adrift with her, another constellation.

A pulse struck Tij, causing her to spin wildly, then the deep cracking sound was felt and heard and Tij felt pressure squeeze around her, causing floating objects to come into contact with her outstretched limbs, each memory had no time to realise before another started, it was a frenzied storm of disconnected moments made impossible to ignore because they were all so familiar.

Every scrap of memory was one she had forgotten, all from someone she loved, she knew this, the familiarity sparked a need within her. Tij reached to grab each object mentally and physically, but it was useless, the speed and rhythm of their impact as she spun made it impossible to gather herself.

The red light from the tunnel above came into view once more, she spun in the weightless atmosphere of the engine, it was further away this time around, a deep-red wound that seemed to be healing as it became dimmed by distance.

The air pressure of the engine condensed further, it felt like she was diving deeper underwater. A spark of brilliant white light put everything in the engine in stark relief. Tij gasped when she saw a thick matt-black liquid pouring into the engine through one of the many cracked windows, still lost in the frenzy of moments nothing felt real, the terror that was creeping up her spine was just one of hundreds of sensations clawing at her mind, seeking recognition.

Another brilliant spark was quickly followed by another, all was burning light or creeping void. Through the strobe of ignited memory, Tij saw that the pollution-soaked objects exploded in caustic white sparks when they came into contact with the void, which edged closer to her, igniting objects of memory as it neared. The objects were pressed in toward her by the shift in pressure, quickening the impact, and through the strobe of exploding memory and the dizzying array of experiences belonging to the people she had loved.

Tij started to look for patterns of Enid, a subconscious need began growing within her, seeking solace from what was surely her last moments. She wanted the image, the sound, the feel, and smell of Enid to keep her company in oblivion.

The flicker of light strobed with slivers of darkness, then all coalesced into a single tone of light. Using the material of the objects' curated memory, Tij's consciousness slowly began to build the shape of Enid, a piece at a time, just a smear of recollection at first but soon the mass of memory was shaped by Tij into a sharper image that floated in the void in front of her. The image of Enid held firm as all other memories were repelled by Tij like an immune system fighting the infection of a fevered patient.

The image of Enid grew from her eyes, the shape of her face began to fill with pale skin, the muscles of her cheek twitched as though talking, but nothing could be heard. Tij smiled as the memories of Enid poured into her from the objects before she directed the stream toward the image, everything was out of sequence but belonged to their life together. Enid was still incomplete, she looked at Tij causing her heart to swell with relief only to sink suddenly when Enid scowled and her still soundless lips thinned in anger spitting wordless fury toward Tij.

The scowl shifted as more memory fell toward the image. Tij pushed around gathering all toward Enid. Her face changed from anger and now appeared pensive and lost. Tij reached out her hand toward her lover and the image recoiled, a single step at first, then as Enid continued to grow, another step followed.

The first touch of the void was ice-cold, suddenly cooling Tij's hot skin like a blacksmith quenches iron with water, her body convulsed in shock and felt heavy and leaden, she was helpless as the image of Enid moved further away, the touch of the freezing void tore Tij's eyes from her lover and she looked down to her feet as the cold void clawed itself upwards across her vulnerable flesh. The freezing sensation drew hurried breath from Tij. Focusing her mind back to herself, she stared down to where the border of flesh and void was framed in shocking cold. Her right shoulder felt its touch and all light was pressed against Tij as the last of the memory-drenched objects ignited, a life of forgotten moments exploded like a nova. Then all was cold and darkness.

The void was familiar, there was so much of Tij in it, so much of her life. Tij was not breathing, beyond physical sense, she was now just thought and feeling. The void was full of borrowed memory, hers and others.

New senses twisted themselves into old sight and sound and Tij could see in the tidal darkness the bright white lines that had formed along what was once her nerves and veins. The light was what she was, no what she is, moments ago. Everything with a memory was burning as a seven-pointed spark. What had been an instant explosion in the physical world, here in the void it was kept bright, as if the memory was a wick and the void served like oil in a lamp.

Tij burnt brightest of all that was around her, her light burnt the void as it drew sparks into clusters, then spinning them into threads all drawn toward the gravity of Tij. Aeons seem to pass as the light edged toward her, each bright thread touched her flesh, burning heat turned to freezing cold as she absorbed all, giving redemption to forgotten moments. The more she took into herself, the brighter she became, memory was fuel. Iridescence brought the silhouette of her last desire into stark relief.

Enid was not moving away; they were both adrift in the void. Tij could see the fear on her face. Without hesitation, she threw out her hands, reaching out, but all of Tij's flesh had been burnt away, what was left was a writhing knot of bright threads, which launched themselves toward Enid. They touched her arms the look of fear hardened on Enid's face as she struggled to move in the void. There was no way to escape, the struggle made Tij's desire to hold her even stronger.

Tij was confused by Enid's reticence. Looking at her lover she could see gaps, memories and form that were absent; Enid was incomplete. As soon as the thought made itself known, Tij exhaled a pulse of light that searched along her threads and all the sparks that were gathered to her. Every memory of Enid Tij had was transmitted along her growing web of light back to the centre and then out along the dozen threads that held Enid.

Injecting the new-found memories of Enid into her, Tij watched with satisfaction as some of the gaps filled like a healing wound filled with blood, but it wasn't enough, so much had been lost in her short time in the star that Tij's template of Enid did not fit, it never did.

The look of fear never wavered from Enid's face, her lips wide and slow as if screaming, the more Tij rebuilt her the more solid she became and Tij felt despair as Enid used now solid limbs to push against her.

Tij knew the image in front of her was a projection, Enid was a collection of light and thread just like her, but Tij's mind refused to see anything but the flesh of her lover, panic and anger emanated from her in waves. Tij grew desperate, sending pulse after pulse of light along her growing network of bright thread and veins. She was so much more now, all light was being drawn toward her, but there was nothing more of Enid.

Desperation turned to fury. Tij knew there was the rest of Enid out there somewhere in the void, the star could not have burnt away so much. Stretching out her threads of light like a web she felt the dust of alien memory become captured, a cold jolt of electricity brought it into her, here were thoughts of people only familiar to her through redemption, their lives lived separately from her. More memory was captured and Tij grew in both light and size, a new star burning in the void.

Frantically searching through the memories in the captured accretion disk of dust, Tij found nothing of Enid, but there was much that Tij adored and admired from the dust of countless lives; love affairs and moments that felt so similar to what Enid and Tij'd had together. It must be enough. It was a desperate harvest taken from the dust from the lives of others.

Tij picked through the alien memories, looking for the right fit, the ingredient that most closely resembled Tij's desire of who she wanted Enid to be, then transmitted her selection along threads that still held onto Enid.

Enid's expression changed, the lips grew still, but it was the eyes, Tij knew the look, she remembered it, it was scorched into her very being, it was a look begging Tij to let her go. But she couldn't, she would never be lonely again, not here in the infinite void.

More dust fell and the star that Tij had become continued to grow, as she filtered through what fell into her gravity, carefully selecting any ideal element that could be used then pushed them along her threads toward the entangled Enid and inject them into her.

Tij saw Enid complete, the memories foreign to both showed as black scars stretching all over her body, her face was mottled, and the hands balled into fists.

Enid was breathing, rapid shallow breaths, fear flowed from her, eyes now animated, they were so much darker and wide with terror, searching the void, all light and motion stopped, and their eyes met. Tij couldn't hold her glare and looked down at herself, all she now was corded knots of burning light, she could see falling dust, the last debris of the star as it fell into them both.

Enid reached out with clenched hands, forcing through the void between them, hitting Tij who felt jolts of electricity and despair from the impact. 'I need you,' were the words she wanted to say, but she had no mouth. 'Come back to me.' No sound passed between them. 'Please,' was transmitted but unsaid.

This last word coiled around the others in strings of deep-red light that floated toward Enid, disappearing as they touched her. The jolts ceased when Enid started to break through the connecting threads.

Desperately, Tij reached out to Enid with more light. Her heart sank as her lover fought to free herself from all efforts of contact. The image of Enid in the void slowly turned away from Tij, panic and fear pulsating from her in angry shades. The last Tij saw of Enid was her beautiful face, tear-streaked, scared by Tij injecting her with elements to rebuild her lover into what she needed her to be, but this was a fabrication, a lie. Once more Tij expected Enid to suffer to love her, but now she had a choice – absorbing the dust of alien memory brought a revelation, Enid felt cold, she had suffered enough. Looking back at Tij one last time, she continued to move away, her dark eyes smoking with hate.

# Chapter 15 – World Consumed.

The freshly carved river of light began where Meco's home ended, he sat with his back to the last standing corner of what was once the receptacle of what little he owned. He pushed his dirty boot through the rubble.

His home was the closest thing he had to solace, but there was no warmth here, no life, no one other than him. In the end his solace had been such a brittle thing made from brick, rock and wood, now shattered, and he did not know how to rebuild it, and even if he knew, he didn't want to.

The river of light, a remnant of the star that had ploughed through all that was his, was dimming, still more of the Blissed ran into it, their molten bodies quenched in turn by the memories held in the light, it was a rebirth. Each one of the Blissed arrived at the river unformed and desperate, and the gift of light they hungrily sought gave them both form and consciousness. It was a miracle, one he had seen countless times, and every time Meco was filled with jealousy and repulsion in equal measure.

The Blissed were not driven by duty or purpose, theirs was an existence designed to explore and learn, to follow the instincts given them by their consumption of light, then live a life where they would forge new experiences and memories for the next harvest. It was the miracle that enslaved them and turned them into what they were – nothing more than a crop to be reaped.

Meco struggled to reconcile his feelings, he always envied the gift of change, to become someone new, to lay everything down and begin again. He hated the Blissed and the way they sought redemption so easily when the memories of their current lives became difficult causing them to burn, glow and suffer. All miracles are cages he thought and spat into the river of light.

The Seeds he understood, suffering was purpose and purpose suffering, they would fight for their lives even though it brought them agony, it mattered, and they would not surrender their lives easily, it had to be taken from them.

Using the wall of his ruined home to stand, Meco felt a thrill of elation.

'There's no more redemption,' he growled, to himself at first then repeating the words, shouted at the top of his voice, throwing them toward the closest group of Blissed like a jagged arrow loosed from a bow stretched to breaking point.

'There's no more redemption, this is it!' He flung his arms wide and grinned at the Blissed closest to him, who were all standing in the light of the river, watching him. None of them spoke or moved a muscle.

'You're all like me now––' A laugh interrupted his verbal assault. He whispered to himself, 'what you are now, this is all you'll ever be.'

Turning, Meco looked at the wreckage of his home, solace, safety, a reliquary of a life lived, this place had been none of those things, it was where he slept, hoping to dream, nothing more.

This should matter to him, he knew what their solace had meant to the Seeds and he had tried to build the same, but you can't build solace from borrowed memories and stolen dreams.

Moving toward what was the centre of the ruin, toward what remained of his bed, surrounded by objects he had collected, just as the Seeds had done. Kneeling down, Meco brushed the soil and splinters aside, looking for remnants of what he had collected. His hands stopped as they touched the corner of a frame. Meco lifted it from the ground and brushed it clean with scarred and filthy fingers.

It was a small painting of someone he had never known, painted by someone he had never met. The subject was a dark-skinned woman in a green dress with long flowing hair, leaning against an apple tree heavy with fruit, her eyes were bright with mischief as she looked out toward the world, her crooked smile told a multitude of stories that Meco could only dream of, and dream he did.

Meco crawled to a standing corner of the house and propped the small painting carefully against the wall. He had long used up the memory this object had once contained, borrowed dreams were just another ruined home.

Carefully treading through the debris, Meco continued his search for more salvage only stopping when a strong wind filled with the ash of the world swirled around him, causing the painting to fall face-first back into the dirt.

There was a pause, and Meco shook his head, his disdain for this false solace was transmuting into grief, it was ridiculous, why would he grieve for a broken home filled with memories of solace that had never belonged to him?

Instinct told him he was being watched. He turned slowly back to the dimming river of light – the Blissed standing in the river closest to him were all watching him. Meco immediately felt a jolt of shame course through him as his moment of vulnerability was witnessed. He held their gaze steadily, his eyes narrowing as he felt one unfamiliar emotion replaced by one all too familiar – anger.

Rushing forward, Meco leapt upon the ruined corner of his house and stood, perched upon it. He could see all the Blissed in the river were looking toward him, all still and silent in their new forms, their features lost in the dying light.

Instinctively, the Blissed feared Meco as sheep feared the sheepdog, but now they stood and waited. Unsettled, Meco climbed to the other side of the wall. The saturated ground gave way, and he slipped down the freshly exposed embankment. The light of the river had not only dimmed but had lowered as it had been consumed by the scores of Blissed. Meco lashed out an arm and a leg, desperate to catch hold of a root or something to stem his fall, but there was nothing that held and

Meco realised in horror that he was sliding toward the river of light, falling headfirst into the light.

Submerged, Meco flailed around wildly, all his senses were obscured by the dimming river; he felt weightless and disorientated. Drawing himself into a foetal position. Meco's right foot touched solid ground, then the left. He slowly rebalanced himself and stood.

The river fell from his eyes as his head broke the surface, his vision blurred but he could still just about make out the rank of the Blissed in front of him. He rushed to get away from them, falling back under the surface as he did so. He flailed with his feet and hands. All he could see was golden light. He squeezed his eyes shut but the light poured into him through his nose and mouth, it tasted of honey and copper, similar to blood but thin and sickeningly sweet.

Meco's hands and feet found the riverbed again. Panic was rapidly spreading through him, his heart raced and he closed his mouth, resisting the urge to breathe. The need to get out of the warm light overpowered him. Meco clawed at the soil, dragging himself from the deeper light to the shore, using his feet and hands to drive him forward. The river shallowed, he stood quickly and clumsily, lifting himself from the water, which was now only stomach deep.

He was numb with fear, senses and instinct swirled around him, a question screamed in his mind – was he going to change, was the tainted miracle of the Blissed to be his fate?

He strode through the light toward the closest bank. The river grew shallow, but his panic deepened.

Launching himself onto the shore, Meco lifted himself to his knees and vomited the light he had swallowed, scowling he spat, then cleared his nostrils. The taste lingered.

Standing, he began manically flicking the light from his body, reacting as if he was on fire. Falling forward onto hands and knees, he vomited again.

Wiping his mouth with a filthy hand he winced, his stinging eyes adjusted and focused, he looked at the back of his hand – the light had gathered in his scars. He checked the other hand and then his arms, all his scars were filled with light.

Meco stood poised, all his senses told him he was wet, not burning, proven by a gust of wind that caused him to shiver.

The eyes of the Blissed did not waver. Meco stood ignoring them, wringing the light from his clothing, desperately trying to rub the light away from his scarred flesh.

'No!' The word was spat from his mouth with the sweet taste of light. He stripped away his clothes and kicked them into the river, looking around for something to scrape himself clean. Finding a broken tile, Meco scraped the light from his skin, revelling in the pain as the edge cut deep into his flesh. Where there had been light between his scars, there was now blood, and he stared back at the Blissed. They watched him scrape the light they so desperately need away from him. Meco dug the edge of the tile deep; the blood that flowed washed away the light. For him, there was never a chance of redemption, the sphere that he sacrificed everything for to ensure its continuance was never for him.

Naked and covered in blood, Meco was breathing so hard he was spitting through teeth that were so firmly clamped together that his face was locked into a rictus grin.

Dropping the tile, Meco began to manically rub his hands across the bleeding wounds on his body, smearing thick blood across his scarred flesh, using it as disinfectant to remove any trace of light.

Finally satisfied that he was cleansed, he paused, he could feel the collected weight of stares from the Blissed, who still stood in the river. He raised his head, the grin still fixed on his taught face. His eyes met theirs. He stepped back, shocked by how many there were, each step he took was matched by the herd of Blissed. Meco's subconscious was pumping adrenaline and information along his mind and nervous system. There were more than a hundred of them, all staring and moving toward him.

He looked for the sharp tile, but he was still stepping backward. The Blissed were on the bank, no more than forty steps away from him, he could see their flesh had cooled and they had solidified into their new forms, their last forms.

The world was darkening; through the herd of Blissed Meco could see what was left of the river of light, puddles, and smears on the dark ground, it was all but consumed. He looked up to the sphere, almost all of the remnants of light were gone, no more constellations stalked the sphere. The only sources of light that remained were fires that still raged across town and forest, the few dimming rivers and the impact wound that the star had inflicted when it left the sphere, which was glowing a bright angry red, casting crimson spears through the smoke and darkness. It shone like fresh pain from a new wound.

Meco raised his bloodied hand and held it next to the red light, watching it glisten.

'Where is redemption, where are we supposed to go?' one of the Blissed called out, her voice pleading.

Meco was surrounded by the Blissed, he could see the fear in their eyes, he could smell it, the light that had given them form could not wash away everything.

He cocked his head to one side, unsure how he would respond. The full repertoire of violence played out instantaneously through his mind, the Blissed sensed this and all but one of the herd moved several steps backward.

Meco laughed as he stalked toward the one Blissed that did not move away, he circled around her, repeatedly feigning an attack on the Blissed that now surrounded them, savouring when they cowered or raised their hands to protect themselves.

Turning his attention to the Blissed at the centre, the one who spoke, Meco saw she was a broad, short, dark-skinned woman with a handsome face and bright hazel eyes that were fixed on him, fear radiated from her, but it was clear from her poise that it was not from him.

'I am Sara.' She put a hand on her chest and spoke in a low, calm voice that waivered only slightly.

Meco saw the gesture as condescending and spat back a taut response: 'And Sara is all you'll ever be.'

Sara lowered both her hands to her side, balling them into fists. 'Where are we supposed to go?' she repeated in a firm, low voice.

Meco moved toward her and placed a heavy hand in mock consolation on her shoulder. He leant in close to whisper in her ear: 'Where does your new form, your new memories tell you to go?' He removed his hand and stepped back leaving a blood-red handprint stain on the tattered white dress she wore, all the Blissed wore them, all were torn but cleaned by the river of light, his mark would be the first of many on this pristine material.

The woman looked down at the stain on her shoulder and impassively returned her gaze to Meco, but the pupils in both eyes had grown large, there was a slight clenching of the jaw.

'I don't know any of this.' Her voice raised an octave. 'I know where I am——'

Meco interrupted: 'And where is that my friend?' He raised his eyebrows quizzically.

'This place is halfway between town and the home of redemption, I know where my home is, it is over there in town, it's burning, everything is burning.' She pointed.

Meco clenched his teeth and turned to speak to the herd that had gathered a step closer.

'This is not the world you were promised?' Some of the Blissed nodded, others shouted their agreement. 'All you have been given are the memories of how to live in a world that already exists, in a new form yes, a new body, new ideas, but the world was always the same, it's always been the same. Revolution has been inflicted upon you,' Meco hissed through a smile, and the Blissed quietened, he turned from the herd back to the woman at the centre. 'You have willingly sacrificed all you were before to the star, for it to burn and light the future, you have done this so many times, not selflessly, let us not pretend, you surrendered a life you had as soon as the memories became painful and started to burn, to hurt.' Meco moved toward the woman in the centre, who stepped back into the herd that was once again moving away from Meco but unwilling to flee without answers.

'Your idea of eternal paradise was an unchanging world, a world you could live within as long as you could change who and what you are, as soon as life became difficult, where the burden of living became painful, you sought redemption and you became someone new, and here you are.' Meco raised his arms and spun around, still smiling.

'You are the one who hunted us if we ran, you forced us to change if we didn't sacrifice ourselves to redemption, I know you.' One of the herd stepped forward, he was a tall man with short hair and dark eyes, he was scowling angrily.

Meco felt some of his anger abate, 'If some part of you remembered running, then you carry memories of a Seed in you now, part of you was someone who chose to suffer, who fought to keep the memories and life they had, that part of you I never hated, you I will tell what comes next.' Meco placed both his hands on the man's shoulders, and he stared into the widening eyes of the Blissed.

'When each of you started to burn, most of you here willingly sacrificed yourself to redemption, to end your suffering, to be given new lives to live in an old world, where all the rules were known, where every morsel of food, every splash of water, even the clothes you wear were provided for you on demand.' Meco returned to the centre of the herd that was closing around him, its ebb and flow that of a beating heart. 'The sphere was dying, it could not sustain you, too many of you ran, selfishly suffering to keep a life they loved to themselves, not to see it burn as fuel, and they suffer still, here you are, intact and whole, complaining and terrified, as the Seeds burn red,' Meco pointed toward the bright red wound, 'that is them burning.' He laughed as a thought came to him. 'Their light is all that will be left in the world soon, there is no redemption, there is no escape, you will have to live and suffer like me, like the Seeds.' Meco stood, listening with satisfaction to the growing panic of the Blissed around him.

'Where is redemption? Find her' a cacophony of fear swept around the Blissed. Meco watched as most ran toward where redemption had once lived, even now at the first sign of doubt and pain they sought release.

'Be free,' he screamed repeatedly, and ran after the Blissed, a crazed shepherd chasing a terrified flock toward the empty house of redemption.

The home of redemption was a large cube of opaque glass with threads of brick. When the glass cleared a skeleton of rooms could be seen, and like the world, it was dark, but unlike the world it was completely intact.

The Blissed were hungry again in their new forms, some for guidance, others for redemption. They broke upon the wall of the structure like waves moving from where Meco stood. A crack resounded through the smoky air – the door had given way, a door that had never been locked had been forced open.

Meco pushed his way forward through the Blissed, each face turned toward him, their desperation burning brightly in their eyes, their lips pleading. Pausing at the open scar of the broken door, the Blissed behind him ceased to push, unwilling to be close to Meco who was seeing the last light of the world reflected in the dark glass wall. The final glow of exhausted fires and specks from the diminishing shreds of light still trapped on the sphere reflected on its surface; the home of redemption had never looked so small.

This step was the first he had ever taken inside Tij's home, every step that followed resonated through the silent house. He was never welcome here, redemption had no time for him, but he knew the house, he had watched the lives Tij had lived many times, he had witnessed the joy and love here, now so clean, and empty.

He closed his eyes and listened as the Blissed poured through the door behind him, he heard them scuffle and cry out, the thudding and smashing of wood and glass. The Blissed flowed around the house like a tsunami, striking every surface and leaving wreckage and chaos in their wake, the air was filled with the sounds of destruction and desperation, each and every Blissed needed to be the first to find redemption.

Meco stood still, breathing steadily through a crooked smile, as he waited for the realisation to hit the Blissed that there was no redemption, he had not lied, he did not need to when the truth was permanent and undeniable, it would be a moment he would savour.

The Blissed stopped and silence fell once again. Meco opened his eyes and saw the Blissed all staring at him, they were a herd with a predator in their midst, and he was all they had to guide them in the world. They waited, all breathing heavily, some crying, all motionless, watching Meco's every move.

Wherever Meco walked, the Blissed parted, revealing the damage they had wrought. He could hear glass and ceramic crush under his bare feet, he felt the edges pierce his flesh, but it was soothing in a way, the pain put him here, in this moment, and that was where he needed to be, he wanted to bear witness to this place, where love had lived and died so many times.

Looking around, he could see he was in the heart of the house. He moved to the wall where the light switch would be. Flicking it on, the glass walls were tinted and the near dark world that had spilt inside was held at bay for a few moments longer. The spotlight in the ceiling stuttered, the Blissed saw the light and stared upward, transfixed. Meco shook his head as he continued to look around. The room was filled with comfortable worn furniture, large sofas and deep chairs, against the glass walls were shelves, floor to ceiling, filled with a vast array of books, papers and boxes, a eulogy of lives lived. Piles of books that had been stacked were scattered across the floor, there were sketches and paintings, photographs ... there was life here, layers of existence and it was cherished, loved.

Meco scanned the faces and images and as he turned bumped into a writing bureau, its lid hung broken. There were piles of letters. Meco picked one that had been folded many times and felt gossamer thin.

Meco struggled to read the worn ink in the flickering light. "To Matthew – we met at the festival of music. We bumped into each other dancing and you spilt your drink and you looked at me terrified. When I laughed you looked so relieved ..."

Meco could not see the middle of the letter, which had worn away, but he could make out the last few lines. "One thousand, two hundred and three times we woke up beside each other, ninety-three we were separate. I locked you away because I couldn't let you go, you wanted to stay at first, then you began to burn and the pain was too much, I knew I would lose you."

The last part struck Meco.

"All that you were is now burning in the star above me. I sit scorched and lonely beneath the death of you."

He read the last words again, gently folded the letter back, and placed it on the pile where he had found it. Tears fell down his eviscerated cheeks, stinging the new scars, washing a small amount of blood. Meco wiped his face with a gnarled hand.

The Blissed stood watching him, implacable in the faltering light. Meco could not hold their gaze and saw amid the ruin of the house of redemption his bloodied footprints.

Meco began to walk into the bedroom, he hesitated, it felt like a betrayal, an intrusion, what Tij had here was alien to him, it would hurt to see it.

Tij was as old as Meco and she had suffered loss, he knew this, but she had so much, so many lives just in this room, a library of a life filled with love, telling of lives lived well. He had been denied even a moment of this, not a single scrap had been given to him. Meco dug into the dark places of the world, he was reviled and feared, he took it because this is how the world survived. Ensuring the future of the sphere was his purpose, peace and rest was his reward, but he had no memory of being held, of laughter or shared life ... nothing ... he had nothing.

Meco buried his rising fury, he wanted to wreck the room, to shatter all that was there. It was rage pure and cold. Before the final atom of rage reached its zenith, Meco saw the corridor just beyond.

Through clenched teeth, he promised the room he would make this place his own, 'I will live here, at least one layer of memory will be mine.'

This room had its own atmosphere, Meco felt its comfort, it was oppressive and began to press down upon him, magnified by the weight of attention from the Blissed.

Light fell into the room from a brightly lit corridor. The Blissed parted as he walked on the light's shadow leading out from the worn, well-loved room. Meco placed his hand on the cool glass wall, feeling along its smooth surface until his hand touched the brick of the corridor. The walls here were painted black, and six doors were painted white, three on either side, only one door was closed.

Stepping further into the corridor reminded Meco of the tunnels he had passed through when hunting Seeds, even the echo of his steps, the feel of the place, was heavy and thick, this was a prison.

Dark atmosphere crept into the corridor from the room, Meco felt fear crawl its way up raw nerves. Gritting his teeth, he forced himself to push into one of the rooms. At first, the wreckage in this room was the same as the rest of the house, but none of the Blissed had set foot in here; he could see them crowded at the doorway, unwilling to be closer.

Everything in the room was scattered, the walls were scorched and the bed against the far side was covered in soiled sheets, the smell of which pervaded around the room, invading his nostrils and throat.

Kneeling down, Meco sifted through the debris, memories of a woman with red hair struck his mind, but it was a life out of sequence, like the tunnels he took to hunt the Seeds, it was a sickening kaleidoscope of a beautiful life, a projection of strobed images.

He continued to move his hand, reading the memories in the splintered objects like brail. A whole life together was burnt into him in moments. He neared the bed and the memories darkened, he saw flashes of Tij leading her here, the woman was burning bright, he watched as Tij repeatedly visited, bringing books and souvenirs of their life together, she was trying to build a cocoon for them, an attempt to engineer a solace so they could stay together. All Meco could feel was the agony of the woman. Tij tortured the woman she loved, forcing her to stay in that form through intolerable pain just so she would not be alone.

Meco recoiled from touching anything else in this room, his naked flesh felt corrupted, he leapt back into the corridor and staggered back to the comfortable room, leaning on the wall as he did so. She put them all through this. He wondered, how could she?

The light bulbs in the room fizzed then died, the only light now was red emitted by the brightening wound in the sphere outside, Meco could see its source through one of the long windows. The dissonance of Tij's home made him feel sick. Pushing his way through the Blissed, he ran and tripped through the door, fell to his knees, and tasted bile at the back of his throat. He wiped his lips with the back of his hand. He could hear the Blissed, who had rushed toward redemption, fall into place behind him. They came to find redemption and it was gone. Lost, they now looked to the man who hunted them if they tried to escape their fate. Meco didn't turn toward them, he offered no words of comfort as he sprinted away from Tij's empty house toward the last light on the sphere and heard the Blissed rush to follow him.

# Chapter 16 – Ex Materia.

Robot leant over the edge of the deep, downward reaching tunnel; the exit wound that had been scorched into the world by the escape of the star. A deep shaft reached downward.

The walls were coated in crystals glowing red. A moment's analysis told Robot that its brightness was increasing. Its camera eyes zoomed down as far down as they could, but beyond an uncertain point the depths became ill defined, lost in light. Sitting poised on the edge, Robot could not see where or if the world had an exit.

Pollution oozed through its tendrils, thick pollution filled with emotion and thought once foreign to Robot was now part of its structure, no less than its diodes and operating systems.

Pulses of fear, jealousy and grief coiled their way along tarnished circuitry like a racing heartbeat – fear caused by the unknown elements of the seed crystal, the unprecedented existence of the tunnel, this great unknown.

The grief was for Control, rooted in the near certainty that it did not survive such an impact, the jealousy was because if it did survive then Control had found a way to somewhere else, somewhere out.

The red light of the crystals was brightening, each one with its own Seed at its heart shone like a red eye, countless in number, they lined the walls as far down as could be seen. Robot could not shake the impression that they were all staring back.

Reaching out three tendrils, Robot placed each on the first few crystals where they started at the bleeding edge of the shaft, cautiously feeling down the crystalline surface reaching half the length of the metal limb.

As the tendrils explored the surface they knocked against a large cluster of crystal. A clean sharp crack echoed from below and Robot watched as a slew of crystals plunge downward, everything they hit broke more crystals loose in a cascade of red flecks of glowing light.

With small diodes, Robot observed the crystals fall, the red eye stared back, soon lost in the dust and haze of the tunnel as it disappeared from view.

Moving its tendrils along the crystal caused sparks, the surface was as flint to Robot's metal as it hesitated.

Each spark flashed images along wires, stories, songs, and thoughts, all new, of lives unlived, these were dreams created when the star cauterised the wound it inflicted when it stabbed deep through the strata of Seeds, now trapped forever singing their songs of solace.

Robot had sowed the area around where the star had hit the surface, it was many seasons deep with the objects the Seeds had taken from the world, infused with the heavy forgotten emotions of pollution filtered from the fuel from countless harvests, cast back to the world, gathered by the Seeds, and taken deep into the surface of the sphere.

This was where Control struck, with a hot bright star stretched into ribbons in ravenous pursuit. Control had driven the power of the whole star into this place, through the countless layers of Seeds, now fused forever into their solace. Old elements and memories had been transmuted into innumerable experiences, new and unfelt. Control was the system and the system removed itself from the world to save it.

New materials are needed to build a new world and here they were. The energy generated from the impact fused the Seeds into crystal, and Robot could only theorise that as the energy spread under the surface of the sphere, all the Seeds and their solace would be transmuted into red glowing crystal.

Between Control and Robot, they had created light from elements rejected by the star as fuel, it would never burn as bright as joy and happiness, but sadness and misery burnt much slower, without the greed of the star and the system it might sustain a world, sadness wrapped in the solace of inspiration and dreams.

The sacrifice of Control had given the sphere a chance of a future. Robot slipped into a daydream for a moment, awash in the pollution of borrowed sadness. It imagined the Blissed mining for light; the light of the crystal was a poor meal compared to that given by the star, but the effort and community that would be needed to delve and collect the light and the collective purpose would perhaps make up some of the difference – a future is built not given, Robot mused, as it spared a moment for a future that it helped to create but would not be part of.

Reaching into its frame it held a matted book in its tendril, pulling it out from its heart, the pages were drenched and would never open, but the story it told would be carried by its pollution. Lifting the book to the place where static crackled from a rudimentary speaker, Robot would not transmit the message as image, it would be the storyteller for the new world, and with a low crackling timbre, spoke into it.

'Control and Robot filtered sorrow, pain and loss from your surrendered lives, we used this to break the soil of the old world, so the Seeds may grow, their sacrifice is greater than our own, the stories of their pain and devotion will light the world. To the Blissed hearing this, you survive us because you are malleable, you will adapt to the new world, do not hide from your misery, the Seeds will light the way.' Robot shifted slightly. 'Redemption had to be removed from the world, there would be no star to feed, but the instinct of redemption, of Tij, would be to continue to save you, the Blissed from pain, but you will all need this pain to drive you, to move forward and find a new purpose for yourselves, there will no longer be a star to feed, to serve. You will need the pain you all ran from, as you now see, joy burns brighter but sorrow burns longer, it is the steady forge needed to create the precious elements of the future. The longer a light burns the longer you will have to evolve and change.'

Pausing for thought, Robot continued: 'I feared redemption would absorb all from the Blissed seeking to flee this strange new world. It could not end well for her, she would be eviscerated by the endless selfishness of you, magnified by desperation and fear. She deserved better. To help her on her journey into the next phase of her existence, and to keep her there in the engine, I planted her in the rich material of her forgotten life. She was to sleep among the myriad of those precious forgotten relics taken from the countless lives she has shared on the sphere, from those she loved. This was to be a refuge, to float at the centre of the sphere, away from the relentless need of the Blissed, where the gentle glow of her existence would serve as a monument to the world in place of the tyranny of the star. That redemption has left the world is my doing, but I confess, I did not foresee that the engine, which was to be her solace, would be tangled up in the ribbon of the star and dragged from the world.'

Sitting on the edge of its known world Robot mused. 'A world without redemption was a world where consequence mattered, scars must be bourn and fear and pain must be faced and endured, the world you will build will be her final gift to you.'

Robot, poised at the edge of the tunnel, book balanced on a single tendril as it looked down into the deep-red depths, once more Robot gave pause.

Tentatively, Robot lowered the static of its voice.

'How could we know the sphere had an edge? I do not understand, my world ends at the bottom of that tunnel. All I wanted for myself is darkness. There would be no redemption in the new world, but there would be change, there would be evolution, people only evolve when there is no other option.'

Robot opened itself, uncoiling every tendril out until it resembled a shrivelled tree bearing the fruits of pollution and memory, drenched objects it could not be without. The star had crashed where it should – transmuting the Seeds and the solace they had built from the pollution Robot had returned to the world, from the detritus cleared from the world, the trash of existence now evolved into a precious crystal that would light the future.

Peering down the tunnel, Robot continued: 'This wound will become a scar of crystal, its light will pour into the world in waves of spark and sorrow, all in shades of red. The rhythm of sound and light will serve as a slow pulse, proof that the body of the world survived the loss of its parasitic soul.'

Placing the book carefully down, safe on a ledge beside the entrance to the tunnel, Robot stretched its tendrils, braced itself on the edge, its form fully open, drenched in the pollution of emotions that was not its own, Robot fell into the tunnel of red light.

Robot fell, its sharp tendrils scratching against the crystalised seed wall. Its rapid descent was met with a storm of sparks created when metal met crystal, a thousand emotions unfelt or experienced before created by the transmutation of Seed into crystal, all raw and sharp and flowing through every tendril, filling Robot's form with energy that sparked between tendrils, as each red eye witnessed its descent.

Every second of the fall was a new life lived and felt, not as metal and wire but as flesh and blood. Robot was lost in the reverie of its hundredth life when it smashed into a ledge where the star had cut the tunnel at an angle before continuing its journey.

All the sparks and crystal broken loose by Robot's tendrils fell with it, spark and speck, together they were constellations descending.

Falling through reveries and new emotion, a flicker book of lives lived were brought to a sudden end when Robot smashed into another outcrop of crystal, its arrested descent hit its sensory diodes first as a dull chime reverberated along its metal frame, followed by a flare of sparks from the impact.

Stretching unfamiliar tendrils, Robot shook itself from the dreams of existence that it had lived in the descent, servos whirred, gears and pulleys creaked where moments ago muscle and sinew used to be, the dream was still ebbing away as remnants of the constellation of spark and crystal fell upon its open frame, sticking to the unguent pollution that covered it, each spark a glimmer of a life lost, trapped in the thick liquid like jewels on ill-fitting clothes.

The air of the tunnel was thick with red dust that obscured the way above. Robot reached a single tendril back to the sundered world, the recollection of which returned to memory along with what Robot was, a polluted servant drenched in experiences that belonged to others, the core of its metal heart, what a poet would call a soul was a thousand lines of code, it was neither, but lost somewhere in between the still fading dream of life and redundant purpose.

Crystal fell from unseen fractures above. The red light filling the tunnel rose and fell in the dust and sparks that hovered in the air, memory continued to return as seeing diodes traced their way down the tunnel above until they were level with where Robot lay. Diodes met its crooked reflection in the crystalline red eyes. It did not recognise itself – a swirl of metal lines spinning out from a square metal frame. It wasn't Robot that sacrificed itself, Robot was unfeeling metal, it was the pollution that inspired its fate, filtered from the fuel from the star, which was now fused with the lives gifted by the descent, transmitted from the crystal walls, itself created by catastrophe, the collision of star and Seed.

Through torn speakers it spoke at its own reflection.

'All I ... I,' Robot repeated to itself. 'All I am is consequence, all I have done is a reaction to that consequence, only in the final descent, did I dream a life unlived by others.' It drew tendrils close around its frame; seeing its reflection it looked so small, but Robot felt content. 'I do not know if I should climb or fall.'

Robot felt a vibration in the crystal outcrop on which it lay, then a crack echoed up the tunnel as it fractured away. Robot fell, one diode focused up to the world, the other locked on the fizzing void below. Robot broke the surface of the void; the darkness was flecked with light and agony.

The void swallowed Robot whole without a ripple on its surface betraying the impact.

Floating, weightless, its tendrils flailing pitifully slowly in the dense liquid of the void, like a drowning insect, pain coursed along frame and wire. What once was inert metal was now saturated in the pollution of discarded emotion made into a richer fuel by the bright new lives experienced through its descent through the tunnel.

Heavy emotion burns like embers, the pollution, as much a part of Robot as metal and wire, was a purer fuel and ignited when it touched the void burning with a caustic bright light that leapt like electricity across every atom of Robot. All thought was lost, no memory, experience or programming, nothing in song or story prepared it for such concentrated agony.

Tendrils began to coil inwards like a spider burnt by flame, the shock forced its sensor diodes wide, the void was not empty, it was threaded through with a mycelial web of orange light reaching outward. The source was two stars, both bright orange and appeared to the suffering Robot as spheres of burning threads. The smaller one orbited the larger, growing as sparks fell into them both from every angle like shooting stars, even aflame, Robot was struck by the beauty of it.

Threads reached out from the larger star to embrace the smaller, all the lines betrayed the evidence of the flow of the void, it was drawn toward the stars, did they suffer as well, Robot wondered as the stars' orbit forced an unseen tide toward it.

The void tide crashed onto Robot's frame causing its burning metal body to grow hotter, the suffering was inescapable and glowed a bright blue, the void fizzed upon contact as it ignited the pollution. The dark fluid passed through the robot's frame forcing every tendril and diode to turn away from the stars, away from the growing web of orange light that was everywhere like the sparkling nerve centre of an impossible creature.

The void forced every agonised extremity and sensor to look back toward the sphere. Robot was being burnt alive, forced to witness, and feel the full extent of the suffering of existence, lived and borrowed. The sphere was a black horizon that fell away. Against the orange threads of light, Robot could see the surface was not smooth, it was pockmarked, with root-like structures reaching out and fizzing with sparks as they touched the void; the sphere was being slowly digested in the stomach of the void, the threads of light causing tides that quickened the erosion.

A tide can drown or save those swept up in it, and here that flow pushed the helpless Robot back toward the glowing red wound of the tunnel, each tide bringing Robot closer to the escape of the sphere that only moments ago it was resolved to escape from; each tide heightened the pain.

A welcome spark was the first indication of Robot's tendrils' contact with the crystal at the base of the tunnel. The inexorable tide brought Robot back to the edge of the sphere. Desperate to be free of the void, Robot grappled for purchase to lift itself free, but the brittle crystal kept on breaking away, landing on the surface of the void, exploding into fizzing sparks.

One tendril pushed through to the tunnel and dug into a crack caused by the falling crystal, two then three tendrils found the same anchor and at last it lifted itself into the tunnel. The void clung to every part of Robot as it strained every servo and burning wire to pull itself back into the tunnel to sit in the gap caused by the falling crystal.

The metal of Robot burnt, fuelled by its precious pollution, the metal burnt blue hot, steam poured from it snaking its way back up the tunnel among the glittering red dust.

Robot's metal cooled and sensory input returned along each red-hot tendril, everything felt constrained as damage reports flicked their way through its corrupted operating system. The last sensor to return was the seeing diodes, only one flickered online and was scratched but zooming in and out to focus, the other, scoured and opaque, only showed a milky light and was useless.

What Robot observed was a thick, polymer-like substance connecting every angle of frame and tendril to the void along silken threads, each filled with veins of orange light. Its first instinct was to brace itself, fear sizzling across raw wires that it would be pulled back into the void.

Attempts to flick the silken threads free only caused them to cross over, forming a complex web that only added to Robot's constraint. Everything the void touched coursed with energy, the crystal transformed from blood-red glow and erupted in bright magenta that shot up the walls of the tunnel. A chain reaction reached upward beyond Robot's view, the dust that filled the tunnel sparked and crackled as jolts of electricity arced between motes. Robot perched inside a small cave in the tunnel and stared intently at the silk of the void, tracing it from the churning pool below along the threads laced with light to where they were attached to corroded tendrils, now burning orange-hot from the transmission of energy caused by the reaction of misery and darkness.

Caught in the silken web, Robot was staring straight down into the void, it was a stark choice, a near impossible ascent or destruction. Evaluating the force of its constraint, a tendril loosened suddenly and flicked the silk of the void at the smooth surface of the tunnel above, and then other tendrils convulsed in the final throes of their utility. Robot assessed that their usefulness would last minutes.

Held in a growing web, Robot lifted its weight, testing the strength of it, and in a sudden flurry of sundered metal lifted itself and reached for one of the new threads above, stretching every pneumatic tendon.

The web fell, separating from the brittle crystal, Robot smashed into the void below, its pollution ignited, the stars still far away were larger now, their veins reached out in all directions, those closest were drawn toward the burning memories of Robot, it felt them disappear, layers of life stripped away.

'No!' it screamed. 'Not like this, not like this, I wanted oblivion.'

The veins of the star delved deeper into memory and Robot flailed, swimming frantically as the last seeing diode sparked and then died.

Blindly reaching upward, broken tendrils dug between smooth, hard crystal. Finding purchase, Robot lifted itself upward. Its few remaining sensors told that its frame was free of the void. One of the tendrils became limp, hanging loose and useless.

The web clung on, the restrictions could be forced, stretching the void into gossamer-thin threads, strong but possible to navigate through. As each tendril broke free, Robot flung a silken thread against the crystal; Robot would climb away from the void, back to the world above.

The sound of the tunnel was different, the vibrations were heightened, sensors detected cracks splintering the walls above, the resonance causing the brittle crystals to shatter.

It would be a race to reach the top, Robot was struck by its need to return to the world, its need to keep what it had found, this new light, and bring it back to the world.

Each stretch brought a tangle of web along with tendril, silken threads drew up the void in which they were rooted, everything connected pulsed with energy, heightening the resonance that splintered the crystal above and below. The light of the tunnel changed from red to bright magenta at the touch of the void.

Robot could not see, only feel, all was energy, and it was growing as it climbed. An electrical storm arced between dust and tendril, crystal, and void. It was in the fraught ascent that Robot felt free, suffering, burning and desperation was fuel, it had a gift to lose and new dreams to share with a world, this legacy will be Robot's redemption.

# Chapter 17 – Binary.

Tij cried out to Enid, but the words came out as sparks, projected through a prism of a heart made transparent by loss.

'I am reduced to light, all I want is to share it with you, why do you fight me?'

Enid stopped but did not turn, her star lit in the halo of a sphere that ignited in sparks at her faint touch, its memories pouring into her in a cascade of razor-sharp white light putting Tij in shadow. Enid replied through clenched teeth.

'I suffered for you, I begged you to let me go and you kept me in agony, using memories as medicine, as bandages for a wound that was terminal. When the relics from our life together were used up, you started filling the parts of me that had burnt away with the leftovers from others. And you're doing it again.'

The image of Enid, standing with her back to Tij, her star growing as the alien memories continued to pour into her, the gaps Tij had tried to fill, the wounds were healing, and she was beautiful.

'I was redemption for a whole world,' Tij began.

Enid was looking back over her shoulder, her eyes burning.

'But not for me.'

Stunned, Tij, floated silently in the void. Enid continued, her voice soft: 'I am one of the Blissed, you knew my nature, memory is an agony to be taken from us, by you.'

'So, our love for each other is nothing more than agony to you?' Tij recoiled all but one of the threads that reached out to Enid.

'In the end, yes.'

'Damn you!' Tij's star now a bright red, flares coiled and fell from her surface. 'The whole world abandoned me, harvest after harvest, and I devoted myself to everyone else's suffering, but what of mine, where could I go to escape my agony? Each time I gave the Blissed redemption I looked into their eyes and saw their pain disappear; I used to be so grateful that I could ease their pain, but I grew to hate each and every one of them for choosing to leave, and I was the vehicle of their escape, from me.'

'I am not eternal.' Enid turned and faced toward Tij, her light a brightening gold, the space between the two stars filled with agitated shades of them both, growing in iridescence. 'I gave a whole life to you and for that you tortured me.'

'I did not,' Tij replied, shocked. Enid's star grew darker and moved into a tighter orbit.

'What would you call it, watching a loved one suffer, knowing there was no cure?'

'I call it love; love is a sacrifice,' Tij whispered.

'It's not a sacrifice if you have no choice,' Enid responded, and she continued to orbit Tij, their light now the same shade of orange.

Grief is not just the loss of someone, it is the refusal to let them go. Enid loved Tij, like nothing else in her short life, and she had suffered for her, she had proven her devotion and it had not been enough. Tij had denied her redemption, keeping her locked away while she force-fed her trinkets and memorabilia from their life together, and now she was repeating the mistake, this time with memories that didn't belong to either of them.

Redemption was selfish in her need, Enid needed to go, it was a natural conclusion to a life fulfilled. Each time Tij came into her locked room – 'I begged you to let me go, to end my suffering,' – the only response from Tij was a transmission of more memories of their life together, they fell into the gaps of Enid like comets.

'It had been a good life, but it was over. I stood by your side as you gave thousands of the Blissed redemption, I watched in awe as you took their memory and pain from them.' Enid spoke using bright radiation.

The transmission from Tij stopped.

'At first I followed you in secret, watching as you gently took them by the hand and led them to the Blissed fields, all I wanted was the same mercy.'

Floating in the void, Enid was incomplete, she could feel this, there was just enough of her to know what was missing, looking down at her body, she moved her hands across flesh she knew could not be there. Her new form was overwhelming, but it was just another form. Enid remembered the first time she woke up in her last life on the sphere, how strange and exhilarating everything was, a new form, new skills and knowledge and a clean slate, bereft of memory or roots, surrounded by so many people all in the same state, it was thrilling.

Two stars orbited in silence. Meeting Tij was a consequence of every life, redemption was inevitable, but before that time Enid had explored and experimented with her new body and gifts – she was creative, a culinary luddite, a hesitant poet and manic conversationalist, she occupied one of the many empty buildings, immediately remaking what was there and adding her own style and relics. She devoted her existence to sharing her life with as many people as possible. These memories were solace to Enid. Tij had joined her in this life, and they created a new one together, like two trees leaning into one another until they were fully entwined.

As their life together grew Enid stood by Tij's side each time she gave redemption to the Blissed until few remained.

It was then, when the world was nearly empty, that her own memories began to burn. It was time to leave and her first approach to redemption was in joy; the completion of a life gloriously lived.

Enid remembered Tij's reaction the first time she had asked for redemption, transmitting this memory across the void between them.

'I came to you, broken and suffering, I limped toward you and held you in my aching arms, holding you close to my burning heart, the heat pouring from my burning flesh caused you to stiffen and pull away.'

'I couldn't hold on; I was too weak. My heart sunk as you stood with your back turned, I could see your shoulders shaking as you cried.'

'Ever so gently, I eased my arms back around you, feeling you relax just slightly when I traced my lips across the back of your neck. I was so happy when you squeezed me close, then I whispered into your ear, 'Thank you for this life, for your love––' You spun around before I could finish, I've never seen you so angry, I could see it scorching through tear-filled eyes, this one look filled me with dread, in that moment I knew you would not let me go.

This memory was a connection between them, a scar they both shared that reached out in a thin delicate thread between the two stars, and it was through this connection Tij continued the story of their memory.

'As your agony grew, you could not leave the house, you told me over and over that every sinew, muscle, breath, and heartbeat was torture. You burnt brighter and still I couldn't let you go. You screamed and all I did was surround you with relics of our life together, praising you for suffering for me, begging you to stay, washing your burning flesh, holding you close. I remember I had to squeeze my eyes shut to protect them from the heat emanating from you.'

Enid responded: 'You gently stroked my hair while I screamed for redemption.'

A red flare erupted from Enid and smashed into Tij. 'You twisted our glorious life into a prison of pain and misery.'

Tij whispered a response, 'The objects and souvenirs from our life together was supposed to be a solace.'

'But it was a prison, built from a life that was gone, pictures of a life already over.'

Both stars orbited in the void. 'I suffered for you, at first because I wanted to, I didn't want to leave you but I had no choice, In the end I was lost to agony, but instead of letting me leave our life together happy and joyful, you built a bonfire of memories around me like a pyre,' Enid screamed at Tij. 'The more I suffered the more desperate you became. Everything revolved around your loneliness, your needs, your loss. I lost my mind.'

'I remember, you were vicious, attacking me each chance you got, you became something else––'

'You made me something else. I was lost, driven to the razor edge of frenzied insanity, a rapid churn of emotion, fear and hate, where who I used to be melted. It did not need to be this way.'

Tij was spinning in the void. 'I wanted to keep you here with me, you endured so much, the more you suffered the more I knew you loved me.'

'Love isn't suffering, its mercy.' Enid's star burnt a quieter shade. 'When you finally gave me redemption, I had never felt such relief, such love, despite the suffering you had put me through ... in the end I knew this was a selfless act, an act of love, and it was in that moment I forgave you. I forgave every ounce of pain and misery that had been piled upon me, and that was the last thing I remembered ... that was supposed to be the end.'

But here I am, thought Enid, floating in the void, a star wrapped in fire, countless sensations and experiences all fusing and breaking apart in my gravity.

The flow of memories fell into Enid in cascades of sparks, she could not see where they came from, her senses were frequencies of radiation that could emit and receive. With these new senses she reached out into the void and touched once more the corona of the much larger star that was Tij, its relentless gravity pulling Enid toward it.

It was then Enid screamed, without a mouth, flares erupting in bright arcs from her surface, which pulsed between pure white and blue, her form fired spears of searing radiation into the void.

Enid was beginning to understand her form, beginning to feel the extent of herself, she knew she was incomplete, she felt the constraint of orbit, it was she who was orbiting the larger star, orbiting Tij, still.

Enid winced as she fought to resist another ejecta of memories from Tij, feeling the impact of each and how they rolled across her bright form until they found purchase in one of the many gaps of her consciousness, like rain collecting in an open wound, even now Tij was trying to build Enid from her own memories, forcing her version of Enid onto her new form. Not again, she could not let this happen again.

Orbits are not constant, they decay, and as the relationship between two objects changes, so does the gravity, as material was sent by Tij to Enid, so her mass increased. Tij was no longer at the centre of their orbit, they began to orbit each other. What Tij sent to capture and sculpt Enid was easy to distinguish – the colour of the invading memories and expectations, they were a darker shade of orange, the colour of embers.

Enid quickly learnt to shape the radiation within her to repel what Tij threw, keeping the unwanted gifts apart and distant from her, leaving the gaps in her form as scars, but everything was captured in her gravity, a ring had formed around her created by memories she had deflected from Tij.

Enid turned to face into the void and arcing flares of orange light erupted from the surface of the star that was Tij, reaching out to Enid in entreaty, the sense of longing was palpable matched only by its force. The flares struck Enid square in her back and she spun, flailing arms to break the connection, more flares followed relentlessly, all filled with desperation and longing.

The void between the two stars burnt intensely bright, the energy generated by the force holding Tij and Enid in each other's orbit, the lovers could no longer see each other, all was lost in light, the threads that stretched from both stars grew thicker and brighter.

With threads of her new bright form, Enid reached out into the void, hungry for oblivion.

Orbits continued to shift, changed by the memories that fell into Enid, cascades of falling sparks adding to the mass increasing the size and power of her gravity, warped by the energy exploding between the two stars.

The thinnest of threads reached out from Enid, leading the way into the darkness, she shuddered as the threads of her light touched the sleeping memories of a broken world.

The sphere, the world they had fallen from, was now a large, withered seed, from which they had both grown out into the void. With threads of light and radiation, Enid felt along its surface, the world was formed from rooms, bound together by roots, stone, brick and memory.

Her light explored the outer shell of the sphere, rooms dropped away into the void, drawn into the gravity of either star. What fell into Enid was alien memory that her gravity would tear apart and make her own, help her to become something new.

Enid was a Blissed, and every Blissed hungered for renewal, a new life, and here was a world full of memory. Her light delved deeper into the helpless world, it pulled more material free, some of it fell into either star, some fell into their orbit adding to the ring that spread from them like a halo around the heart of the stars.

As Enid dug into the sphere, rooms and relics fell from the world and she consumed them greedily, already she could feel the gaps in her fill, the memories ripped apart by her gravity were from a generation long lost to time, a desiccated strata ignited by Enid's touch filled her mind with dreams and story, these in turn transmuted to new thoughts and perspectives, she was changing.

Tij reached out again with a single flare, gentler this time, trying to distract Enid who she could see tearing into the sphere. She knew the appetite of the Blissed, equal to that of the parasitic star she once served. Duty and desire aligned, she would not let the sphere be consumed, in doing so she would save both the sphere and her lover.

Using the gravity between them, Tij forced herself between Enid and the sphere she was ripping apart sending the sphere outward into a deeper orbit, beyond the ring that had formed around them.

Their orbits so close they were almost touching, spinning around each other faster and faster, driven by gravity and desperation, the very shape of the two stars warping as their separate coronas fought against each other violently, Enid's fire in shades of red, Tij's dark orange, mixing and swirling into the void, igniting the ring of debris, spreading light and gravity deeper into the void.

Enid, her need for change, for oblivion, for release was once again being denied her by Tij, the sphere was hidden behind Tij there was no way to get to it but through.

'I can't let you––' Tij did not finish. Enid, larger now, piled radiation, light, heat, and soul toward Tij in a series of massive piercing arcs of energy that skewered Tij, rending material, which she consumed rabidly, driven by hunger and fury.

Enid, now even greater in size struck Tij again, gorging on her light.

'Once more you stand between me and redemption.' Enid spat the words.

Wounded, every illuminated atom screaming in pain, Tij whispered her response: 'I can't let you destroy what we built together, take from me what you need.'

The ring that orbited them burnt with a magnesium brightness, filled with memories and relics, ignited by the stars as they fought, its light and gravity trickled through the void as the two stars spun rapidly in silence. Other broken worlds were drawn toward them from the darkness.

All was white light and burning agony, the two stars orbited blindly. Tij's scream hit Enid as radiation, her terrible suffering was all too familiar, Enid knew this pain. She felt the radiation of Tij's anguish wash over her. A hesitant smile of wry satisfaction spread slowly across her face, at last she understood. The screaming continued, striking Enid in pulses.

Broken worlds floated closer, carried by the void tide, inexorably drawn by the new light and gravity of the two stars, the closest was half the size of their home sphere, this world was already split in half, long dormant, filled with desiccated and ancient memory that exploded in a searing nova as it touched the edge of the ring.

The nova was the full spectrum of every colour, every note resonated in a single cacophony that struck both Enid and Tij. Both stars spun, lost in a greater light.

Tij flailed wildly, Enid felt her movements as radiation that hit her in waves of vibration, memory was falling into them both in a downpour of kaleidoscopic comets as they burnt together in the nova of a broken world, penetrating, searing, like white-hot needles. So much of her short life had been pain, all of it in the presence of Tij. Blind and deaf, all senses were reduced to searing pain and the radiation that emitted from her hidden lover was all that was left of their connection.

Enid remembered her suffering, offered as absolute devotion, she also remembered it turning to anger when Tij refused to redeem her, to concede to the inevitable, to free her, wrapped in the purest memories of their life together. She would have left that existence joyously, prepared and grateful, but she was kept and held, even beyond her own voluntary suffering. Now here they were together, in new forms yes, but saturated in their old life.

The intensity of the nova was drilling deep into the star that was Enid, tearing through the form that had been built for her by Tij. There would be no other form, no life to follow this one, this was oblivion at last.

A chord of radiation struck Enid from her reverie, tinged by desperation, history, and selfishness, it was a long deep vibration conveying a single word – 'Please.'

Enid wanted oblivion to rend and tear and butcher a life that had turned into torture, but the word held, it was a hook on a line, and she was caught. This was the word she herself had uttered so many times, a euphemism for release from pain. Her pleas had been ignored.

Twisting, Enid tried to escape. The note changed and along this new connection poured all the fear from Tij. The vibration changed again, it was a high tone of desperation and loss, here was a loneliness darker and more absolute than the void they had fallen into together.

This chord resonated with her anger and pain, it was different yes, but just as deep and powerful, it was excruciating, the equal of anything Enid had endured.

She had not known, Tij had spoken of her misery, but Enid had never known the depth of her grief, there was generations' worth of loss transmitting from Tij, pain brought honesty, here they suffered as equals.

The comets of memories continued to impact; Enid felt herself calm as her anger abated, she loved Tij, the single chord that connected them carried this bright note back to her lover.

The chord pulled suddenly, then eased in severity to gentle but insistent. Enid steeled herself to resist but they had a pure connection, stretched taught between both stars, a high note of need played against the deep notes of their history and the music between, nothing was hidden now, they spoke in a conflicted harmony of beats and rhythms, furious and nurturing, radiating in the need for forgiveness.

Through the searing light they touched, both still blind as their orbit reduced to nothing, the two stars spun rapidly, both distinct entities but now fused.

Their orbit quickened, harmonised radiation dispelled the nova of light caused by the explosion of the broken world, the void became a frame of their rebirth, the void tide trickling into the space the light left behind. It was a cooling presence serving as connecting tissue between light, star and sphere. The still bright nova gathered around them, falling into swirls of nebula in shades of purple and blue, a solace of new constellations and stories, falling gently onto the lovers, bringing a new life. Redemption is not forgiveness, it is forgetting, they would both be someone else in time, how they loved each other would change, but they would always be swept up in each other's orbit.

Together they would face broken worlds, drawn to their light from the darkness, shattered, ruined and wounded, these worlds would be rendered and torn by the gravity of the binary stars, what does not feed them will gather in orbit, an accretion disk of memory-filled rooms, to crash, gather and reform into new spheres, new life.

None on the sphere they called home would see this heaven forged from forgiveness and broken worlds, but they would feel its light, they would share its future.

# Chapter 18 – The Witness and the Heretic.

Darkness crept around the world, the bright rivers had all been consumed by the Blissed, fires that had scorched the world had died down to low embers. The last light that bled into the world was deep red, emitted from the glowing wound, which drew all life on the sphere toward it like a beacon.

Meco ran from redemption's empty house with the Blissed in his wake. Fighting through leaf, branch, smoke, and darkness, the Blissed followed clumsily in his shadow stepping through the thick woodland that was dense with fauna hidden in the darkness, their screeching calls merged into waves of desperation and fear that swirled through the heavy air like brambles.

Meco did not slow, his heart was racing, his naked scarred flesh was covered in new blood. He forged a path; all prey now followed the hunter.

The bitter taste of ash filled Meco's mouth. He broke through unseen branches and finally paused for breath. He could hear the Blissed exhaling air and complaints around him. They stopped and waited, listening, and whispering as they bumped into each other.

A wing of birds scattered from the trees into the unseen above, this sound, familiar and normal, hit Meco like a splash of cold water. He could feel the eyes of the Blissed as he waited for silence.

Warm winds shook the leaves, Meco stood and looked at the world around him, through the gaps in the smoke he could see the eyes of flocks and herds reflecting the dying light back at him. Further away, across the sphere, were constellations of Blissed, the ones still bright and hungry. He watched as they sought the last scraps of the rivers of light. He shook his head, it had almost all been consumed. These constellations were lost and burning, adrift in a dark world they did not understand.

Meco shivered, naked and smeared in his own blood, it was the first time he had ever remembered feeling cold, with the ever-present star there had always been heat, even the fires ignited by its exit from the world warmed the sphere for a time. He could hear the racing heartbeats and heavy breathing of those around him, beast and Blissed. He listened as the rhythms of panic and fear found the gaps between breaths of wind and scorched branches.

Silence fell and the colour from the wound switched from dark red to bright magenta; Meco nodded his head as if in agreement, it was just another change he didn't understand. Watching through tear-filled eyes at the new shade, noting that the new colour did not reveal the dim parts of the world but sat heavily on every surface like a ragged blanket.

The blood covering Meco's body glistened darkly, the Blissed gathered around him cautiously, the beasts stayed in the shadows, birds flocked and settled on overhead branches, he could see indistinct shapes gathered in the bracken, the scant light reflected in their eyes, all watching him.

Nothing was said, the wind continued to blow. Meco broke the silence, speaking through gritted teeth, but only to himself, 'All I am ... all I was ... is gone. All I had was purpose, everything else I forgot, my life became lost to me ....' He paused, deep in thought. The hazel-eyed Blissed called Sara took several steps toward him and Meco recoiled as he continued. 'What is left of me is useless, so why do you follow?' These last words were barely above a whisper that only she would hear.

Sara reached out a hand, which Meco stared at as if it were a weapon. She touched his shoulder, causing him to shiver, and with a slight smile said: 'You cannot force anyone to follow you, they must choose, and our choice is darkness, or you, and I fear you less than darkness.' She moved her hand to his and gripped it tightly. 'And like you, I have nothing.'

Meco looked around at the world and what it had become: cinder, shadow, and alien light.

Sara touched his face. 'Why do you have so many scars?' She asked. Meco was still scanning the ruined world around him as he replied, 'This is what happens when you don't get out of the way.'

'Of what?' Sara began to stroke Meco's face gently.

'Of anything,' he replied.

Sara reached up with both hands and turned Meco toward her. Dark bloodshot eyes met her bright hazel ones. Sara traced the scars on his face. 'It's like Braille, this is the story of you.' She closed her eyes. 'Every scar is a blessing, evidence of a life lived.'

Meco, opened his mouth, but the words would not come. Sara felt the muscles of his face twitch. She reflexively lowered her hands and stepped back.

'This world has carved a cage in my flesh, but I don't remember why.'

'Like every blessing, it is armour.' She was looking at the soft dark skin of her arms and touched her own face. 'I need my own scars,' she said.

'You will have them, the world is full of jagged broken things hidden in the darkness, these things will shred you.' Meco's reply was flat.

Sara was frowning. 'This makes you happy?'

'Yes, we are alike at last, we share the same fate, I won't be alone.'

Meco looked at Sara's kind face and felt her tense as she read the array of thoughts flashing behind his eyes, a maelstrom of emotion and reaction, pumped by a heart that now beat slow.

'I don't know what we will find, I am hoping for oblivion,' he said.

'I know.' Sara held onto his hand. He kept his fingers straight as he guided Sara forward alongside him and returned to walk toward the new magenta light. Their entire existence had been spent beneath the tyranny of light, now they followed its last ember.

Edging through the trees into the clearing, the magenta light glowed fiercely. Sara released his hand and covered her eyes; it was not just its brilliance but the heat that emanated from it. The glowing wound in the surface of the sphere was smaller than Meco was expecting, but he knew that is often the way with lethal wounds.

Meco took halting steps forward, and in his peripheral vision saw the Blissed stop following him and gather closely together, peering around the trees furtively. He could hear branches snap and brambles shake as the beasts of the sphere bore witness.

He did not cover his eyes as he approached the source of the magenta light, even when tears began to stream down his face from the heat and light, which thickened the air around him, flowing across his naked flesh in dense waves.

Low skittering sounds echoed from the depths of the hole, the sound of metal scraping on glass, which grew louder as he reached the rim.

The heat and light were unbearable, but he had to see for himself, he had to witness where Tij had left the world. She surely must be gone; how could anyone survive such an impact?

Looking down, squinting through bright magenta to see if there was any wreckage, the only thing he saw was a tunnel of magenta crystal stretching out below him. The crystals closest to the rim glowed and Meco knelt down to touch them, as there heat touched his fingers a frantic harmony vibrated through to his very bones, he became immediately saturated in a dissonant chorus of emotions, he felt both sick and elated, inspired, and terrified as notes shifted back and forth from dirge to melody. The dissonance was like a tide; it both soothed and eroded Meco's mind.

An image of a huge crystalline root system coursed into Meco; he could see countless Seeds forever trapped in what was once their solace, now transformed into a crystalline prison, translucent and brittle, burning with an alien magenta light. The Seeds were all looking up at him from the deep places of the sphere, their faces twisted in fear, not of him but of the growing light, which was impossible to escape.

A loud crack thundered from the tunnel, splitting the crystal under his hand, snapping him out of his reverie.

Meco drew a sharp breath, stunned by what he saw: crawling up the tunnel was the robot dragging a web of velvet darkness in its wake, and where the void's dark strands touched the tunnel, the crystal ignited into a searing shade of magenta that fizzed inside Meco's mind, drowning out the screams of the Seeds.

Meco tasted metal as he was struck by the ascending morass of the robot, knocking him through the air to land heavily on his back, even when the breath was struck from his body, he never took his eyes from the robot at the head of the web as it burst into the sphere.

The Robot breached the surface and the web continued to grow around it, drawn from the tunnel like silk from a worm. The black threads were almost indistinguishable from the robot's form, the only difference was the strong acidic smell that filled the air carried by the steam that rose from the metal.

A scab of pulsing web and corroded metal formed over the wound in the sphere that was the tunnel. Meco scrambled backwards along the ground. He could see, stuck between the webs, fragments of red crystal. The whole structure resembled a twisted dome of stained glass that convulsed like an exposed heart.

Raising himself off the floor, Meco leant forward on the balls of his feet, revelling in the searing heat as it burnt his exposed flesh. Tears streamed from his eyes, but he did not shield them, unwilling to blink, ready to react to whatever would follow. All he had experienced since star fall was terrifyingly new, but some instincts honed in the old world still held true.

Primed but powerless, Meco mumbled to the beating morass in front of him, 'Everything I have ever known that did not serve my purpose has been lost to me, all I remember is now useless. Because of you. I am not free, you've destroyed me.'

He watched as the robot, splayed across the dome, pushed itself through the web. Its tendrils moved and stretched the morass. Meco could see lines of yellow light shifting within the web like veins through taut muscles.

Like a spider, the robot worked its way through the sticky black web shadowed in the bright magenta light, its tendrils continued to dissolve, some snapping loose only to be caught hanging in the web like a captured insect before disappearing completely with a hiss and a wisp of green cloud as it was consumed by the toxic darkness of the web.

The robot faced Meco, a single broken glass bead hung limply like the last flower of a scorched bouquet, this was the only indication that it was looking in his direction. The wind gusted toward him, carrying the gentle crackling sounds of cooling glass and the acrid smell of liquified metal.

Meco's eyes were now fully adjusted, all his tears burnt away. He started to distinguish between web and the spider-like tendrils of the robot, what remained of its metal frame was ruined, splayed wreckage of spent material was being eaten away before him, the web remained smooth and taught, vibrating in the air. Meco felt no pity, he remembered the sheer weight of the robot as it had pinned him down, stabbing into his flesh, merciless and efficient. The effortless way it had dominated their last meeting was still raw, the wounds still fresh. The robot was a corroded skeleton, fizzing in the black void-like web, though undoubtedly blind, Meco felt it was watching him.

There was no escape, Meco could see that now, even if it was intact the robot would not be able to spring forward and eviscerate him again, what was left was brittle and frail. Meco stood and took a few tentative steps toward the web, both hands clenched into fists. He was only an arm's length away and Meco could see through some of the larger crystals caught in the web. He whispered as he edged closer to one of them and asked, 'Why did you return?'

There was no response as Meco approached, the heat did not relent and was accompanied by a vibration that he felt in his teeth and bones. He moved his head closer to one of the larger crystal fragments, not shifting his eyes from the robot until his cheek pressed against the crystal, it was cool to the touch but vibrating fiercely. Taking a breath, Meco looked through the shard of red crystal and down into the tunnel.

The walls of the tunnel were spirals of cracked crystal all emitting what he knew must be bright magenta light. The tunnel was intersected by dark threads, and creeping its way up them was a thick, dark mass laced with gossamer-thin veins, everything was coloured a metallic pink through the lens of the red crystal.

As the void rose, the crystals it touched erupted ever brighter. The vibration continued to surge through Meco, carrying intense sound and images, a potent radiation that now poured into the sphere. Meco grimaced, struggling to regain focus. He turned to the robot: 'Where is Tij?'

A single tendril forced its way free of the web, it fizzed and reached toward the ground at Meco's feet. Defying the instinct to snap the brittle metal appendage, Meco calmly stepped aside as it shifted through soil and debris. The tendril split then coiled around a book, which it lifted up, pulling it toward what was left of the robot's frame. A dull crack split the web around the robot and a thick black liquid poured through the gap, the golden threads coiled and swam beneath its surface, Meco was mesmerised, and then, slowly and gently the robot drew the tendril and the book into itself.

In the chaos, Meco watched as the robot tore itself apart, wringing the last of the unguent pollution from the wreckage of its frame, he saw the robot fight to keep the void from touching the lifeblood of its pollution, the last of which ran down a single tendril that held the book, which the robot held out toward him.

Looking down at the dripping-wet book, Meco saw the last metal of the robot eaten away by the web, which oozed and slid into the gaps that the robot once filled; the shape of the scab changed imperceptibly.

Meco caught the book as it fell from the metal tendril as it finally dissolved. He closed his eyes and shivered despite the heat of the magenta light, waiting for the message, the story that the book must surely hold.

There was no image, or story that made itself known, there was only a low hum of whispered static that vibrated along his bones, a tactile transmission of voices shattered into disordered kaleidoscopic atoms that resonated beyond his understanding, this message could only be felt, not told, and he did not know how.

'This is your answer?' Meco said and snorted. 'A book that cannot be opened, filled with voices that cannot be heard.' Anger, grief and fear rushed through Meco, his heart began to race once more, his skull felt as if it was shrinking, trying to contain a mind that was swelling with pain and desperation.

Meco laughed manically, tears pouring from eyes shining with magenta light, the futility of his existence finding form in this release. He threw the book behind him, hearing it thud on the floor, the fluid that saturated the book clung to his hand, long thin threads still connected them together, the inaudible voices now little more than the sound of gentle rain on sand.

Mania grew from his heart, speeding along every vein, coiling upward from the hidden vault deep inside him, stored here was the well-earned trauma of a long, lonely life that now flowed within his blood like a raging torrent, engorging the muscles of his throat, choking him, forcing the breath from his ancient, ruined body. He spun and flicked his hand, but the thread would not release him. Meco dragged his captured hand across the ground, soil, dust and specks of crystal became caught, then absorbed making it more solid and heavy and the threads brittle. Finally, they broke free, the vibration ceased, and his laughter abated. The ground shifted beneath his feet.

Cracks split around the scab, impossibly deep, they continued to spread and widen, each filled with bright crystals releasing searing magenta light into the world.

Meco saw a group of Blissed rush forward, basking in the light, sacrificing their brief lives, the broken world too much for them, their forms melting as they danced in the absence of pain and purpose. Meco bit his lip in disgust, the copper taste of blood mixed with bitter tang of jealousy.

A thin mist of dust fell back upon the riven ground, a blend of soil and sparks thrown into the air by the robot's ascent glittering as they descended. Meco was taken aback by the terrible beauty. He breathed sharply as a sharp crack split the ground beneath his feet causing him to fall backward into the scab. He screamed, his back and legs now stuck in the web burnt his skin. Meco did not even have time to blink before the void poured over him.

I end in darkness and the world ends in light – the visceral pain of his skin bubbling in the acidic embrace of the void surrounding him sliced across this realisation, Meco couldn't breathe, all senses were severed from a mind too filled with agony to care, more than anything, he hoped the gift in the darkness was oblivion.

A gentle glow grew in front of his closed eyelids, his skin was suddenly cool and tingling and the pain was gone.

'No, please no.' He was filled with an absence so profound that he grieved the pain. Meco shivered in the grip of this cold yellow light, he could feel hairs rise on the backs of his arms, which had been scorched away in the searing heat moments earlier. Muscles convulsed; each contraction forced more poisonous pain from his body and washed it away in the rejuvenating light.

Meco's breath became sharp and deep, drawing more of the cool yellow light into his lungs – it tasted of watered down honey and stung as it cleansed whatever it touched with clinical precision, cruel words said and heard were erased, the toxic air of hate and jealousy that sustained him, needs and dreams unspoken were gone. The wound that was his heart was healing.

Meco's nervous system carried the fresh cold yellow light around his body, its healing chill an antidote from the heat of the burning world spiralled its way up to his brain where it slowed, creeping around its edges and touched his optic nerve; he finally could see.

Dark void and yellow veins inverted before his eyes, rough black lines scratched into a yellow background spread away from him in chaotic overlapping layers, one strand started to move then another, the shapes forming and reforming into a moving picture showing him the connecting mass of veins collected in the scab, reaching down the tunnel like the trunk of a great tree.

The scratched lines were hard to read at first, then their frenzied motion settled into a still image, that fizzed slightly, giving the illusion of motion, compelling him to follow. Drawn downward, Meco could see the connections between the cracked crystal and the Seeds, which he now saw as the branches of a tree stretching beyond his sight deep into the soil of the sphere.

Deeper downward, the scratches formed into an image – the root system, impossibly wide, whorls of heavy dark matter falling toward the centre where two stars orbited one another. Thin lines, impossibly dark, connected them both to everything.

The lines of the image snapped and shattered, freezing for an instant before rushing toward Meco in a dense constellation that was pushing him back to the scorching world.

Meco fought to push back into the cool healing light with flailing limbs, his tired muscles fuelled by rage and mania.

Meco could feel his skin begin to bubble and blister once again as he was pushed from the yellow light back into the voids embrace, his desperate screams nullified by the darkness. Suddenly a strong hand grabbed his and pulled.

Meco dropped from the void with a thud as the last scraps of yellow light fell away from Meco like after birth. The shock of the absence of heat and light caused him to convulse and shiver, every muscle, nerve and fibre readjusting to the air of the sphere that was so impossibly hot. His eyes came slowly into focus, he looked at his hands and saw all the blood and dirt had been washed away from burnt blistered flesh. Rubbing his hands over his body hurriedly, Meco breathed a sigh of relief that the scars remained, both new and old.

A loud fizz caught Meco's attention. Looking across the void, he shook his head and frowned darkly as he watched a herd of Blissed, some of those that had followed him, drop to their knees on islands between the new cracks in the soil surrounding the void. They were awash with the magenta light seeping up from the crystals below, most were dancing, their forms indistinct and molten. The cause of the sound was when a Blissed hurled themselves into the void, like insects into a flame.

Meco's frown deepened into a scowl as the Blissed threw themselves onto the web, hanging there like decorations, along with the crystal fragments. Veins of light were drawn toward them, blending with their molten forms, bleeding their forms across the surface of the void in rivulets of gold.

The ground cracked beneath Meco's feet; thin lines spread along the ground from the void toward the woods in front of him.

Hiding in the woods were a dozen Blissed, Sara stood right in front of him. Meco's long shadow was cast by the magenta light across her and the trees. He clenched his hand repeatedly and she nodded.

'It was me,' she said and tentatively stepped toward him, carefully staying within the boundary of his shadow until she faced him. Her skin was dirty, and she breathed short shallow breaths, she was terrified, but here she stood.

'Your shadow is our solace; will you stay for us?' The ground beneath Meco cracked causing him to step to one side, leaving Sara exposed to the magenta light.

Her features began to melt, her eyes flicked briefly toward the void before turning back to Meco. She stepped into his shadow.

Sara reformed in front of him, her features returned unchanged, and in this moment, he was her solace from light. He could see that she held the robot's book tucked under her left arm. She once more took his scarred hand in hers and led him away from the void.

Meco felt the light burning into his naked back as he walked, listening to the rushing wind swirling around him that carried the cries of the Blissed. Together they reached the trees; Sara leant against the sheltered side of a blasted yew and spoke to Meco.

'There is something here from the robot to you.' She lifted the book slightly, he responded with a fierce look, but she did not waiver, she continued. 'The chapter begins: The shallow matrix of absolutes. "I fell from the world and played the silken threads of the void, like a musical instrument. I am finally a part of the light you see ..."'

Meco placed his hand on Sara's shoulder to stop her, his bloody handprint was still there from when he first touched her.

'That is not for me,' he said firmly.

Sara smiled. 'The answer to your question is here.' Placing her hand on top of his, moving her face so close he could feel her breath, she whispered, 'Tij and Enid burn brightly in the void, as must we all.'

The ground cracked loudly behind them; the intensity of the magenta light increased as the void bled through the scab, creeping inexorably into the world.

# Afterword

To those who suffer
    If you must sing suicide psalms,
    Master the tune.
    Suffer for those who cannot.
    Swim hard against the flows of greater things.
    Suffer for those who will not.
    If you must be the wick in the candle of your own demise,
    Be a lighthouse, not a hearth.